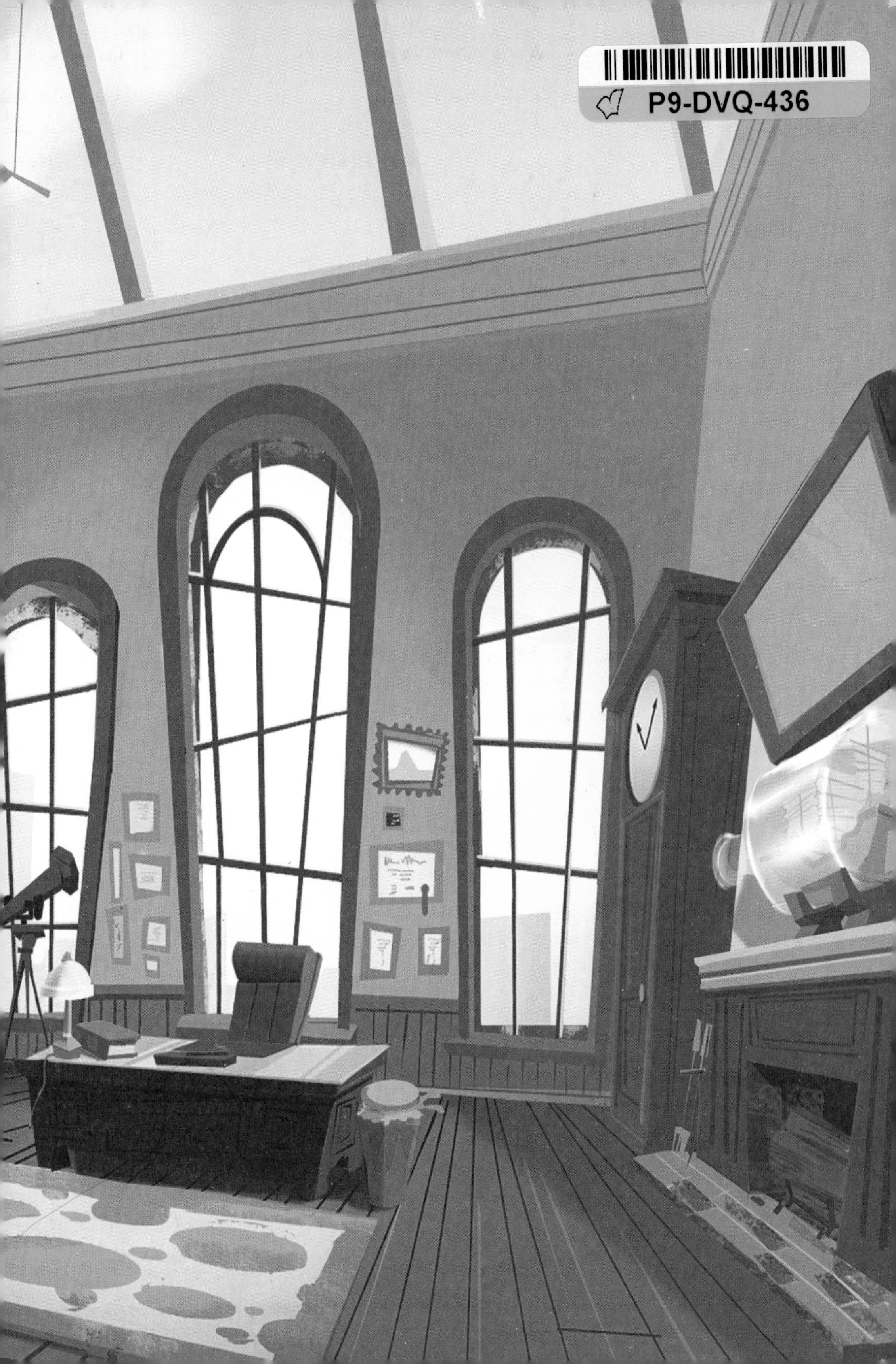

Geronimo Stilton™ Reporter

PAPERCUTZ™

Geronimo Stilton

GRAPHIC NOVELS AVAILABLE FROM PAPERCUTZ™

...ALSO AVAILABLE WHEREVER E-BOOKS ARE SOLD!

#1
"The Discovery
of America"

#2
"The Secret
of the Sphinx"

#3
"The Coliseum
Con"

#4
"Following the
Trail of Marco Polo"

#5
"The Great
Ice Age"

#6
"Who Stole
the Mona Lisa?"

#7
"Dinosaurs
in Action"

#8
"Play It Again,
Mozart!"

#9
"The Weird
Book Machine"

#10
"Geronimo Stilton
Saves the Olympics"

#11
"We'll Always
Have Paris"

#12
"The First Samurai"

#13
"The Fastest Train
in the West"

#14
"The First Mouse
on the Moon"

#15
"All for Stilton,
Stilton for All!"

#16
"Lights, Camera,
Stilton!"

#17
"The Mystery of the
Pirate Ship"

#18
"First to the Last Place
on Earth"

#19
"Lost in Translation"

#1
"Operation Shufongfong"

papercutz.com

Geronimo Stilton™ Reporter

#2 IT'S MY SCOOP!
By Geronimo Stilton

PAPERCUTZ™
NEW YORK

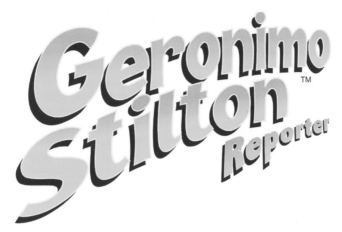

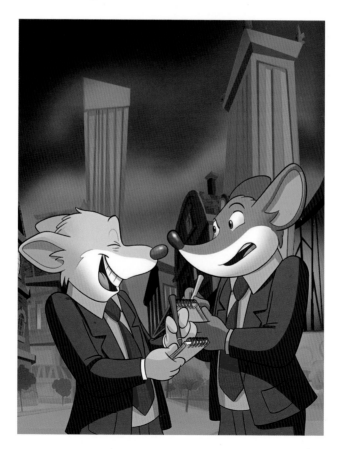

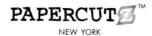

IT'S MY SCOOP!
Geronimo Stilton names, characters and related indicia are copyright, trademark and exclusive license of Atlantyca S.p.A.
All right reserved.
The moral right of the author has been asserted.

Text by Geronimo Stilton
Cover by Alessandro Muscillo (artist) and Christian Aliprandi (colorist)
Editorial supervision by Alessandra Berello (Atlantyca S.p.A.)
Editing by Lisa Capiotto (Atlantyca S.p.A.)
Script by Dario Sicchio based on the episode by Tom Mason and Dan Danko
Art by Alessandro Muscillo
Original lettering by Maria Letizia Mirabella
Color by Christian Aliprandi

Based on an original idea by Elisabetta Dami
Based on episode 2 of the Geronimo Stilton animated series, "Che scoop, Geronimo!"

www.geronimostilton.com

Stilton is the name of a famous English cheese. It is a registered trademark of the Stilton Cheese Makers' Association.
For more information go to www.stiltoncheese.com

JAYJAY JACKSON—Production
WILSON RAMOS JR.—Lettering
KARR ANTUNES—Editorial Intern
JEFF WHITMAN—Managing Editor
JIM SALICRUP
Editor-in-Chief

ISBN: 978-1-5458-0537-4

Printed in India
May 2019

Papercutz books may be purchased for business or promotional use.
For information on bulk purchases please contact Macmillan Corporate and Premium Sales
Department at (800) 221-7945x5442.

Distributed by Macmillan
First Printing

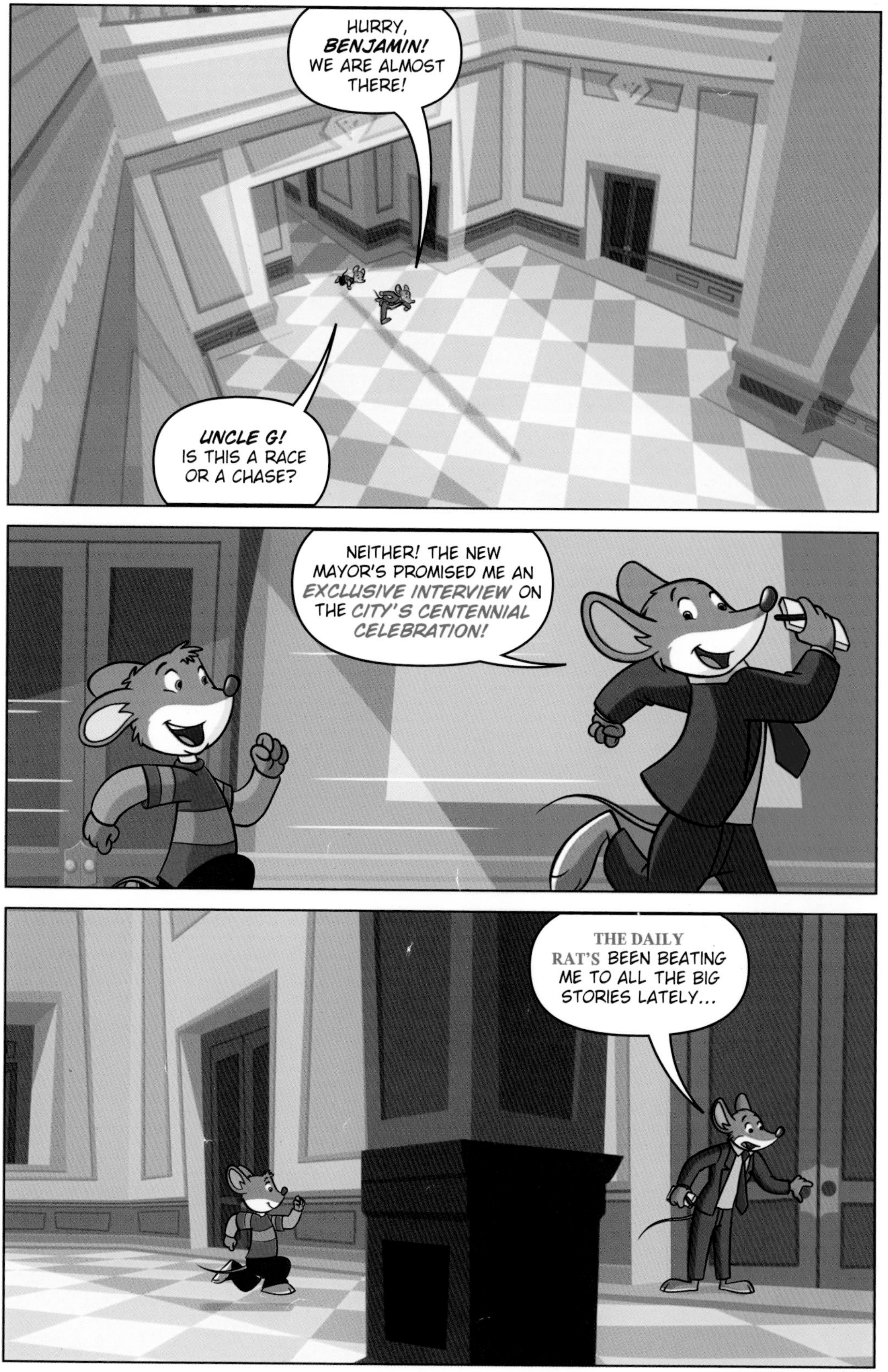
HURRY, BENJAMIN! WE ARE ALMOST THERE!
UNCLE G! IS THIS A RACE OR A CHASE?
NEITHER! THE NEW MAYOR'S PROMISED ME AN EXCLUSIVE INTERVIEW ON THE CITY'S CENTENNIAL CELEBRATION!
THE DAILY RAT'S BEEN BEATING ME TO ALL THE BIG STORIES LATELY...

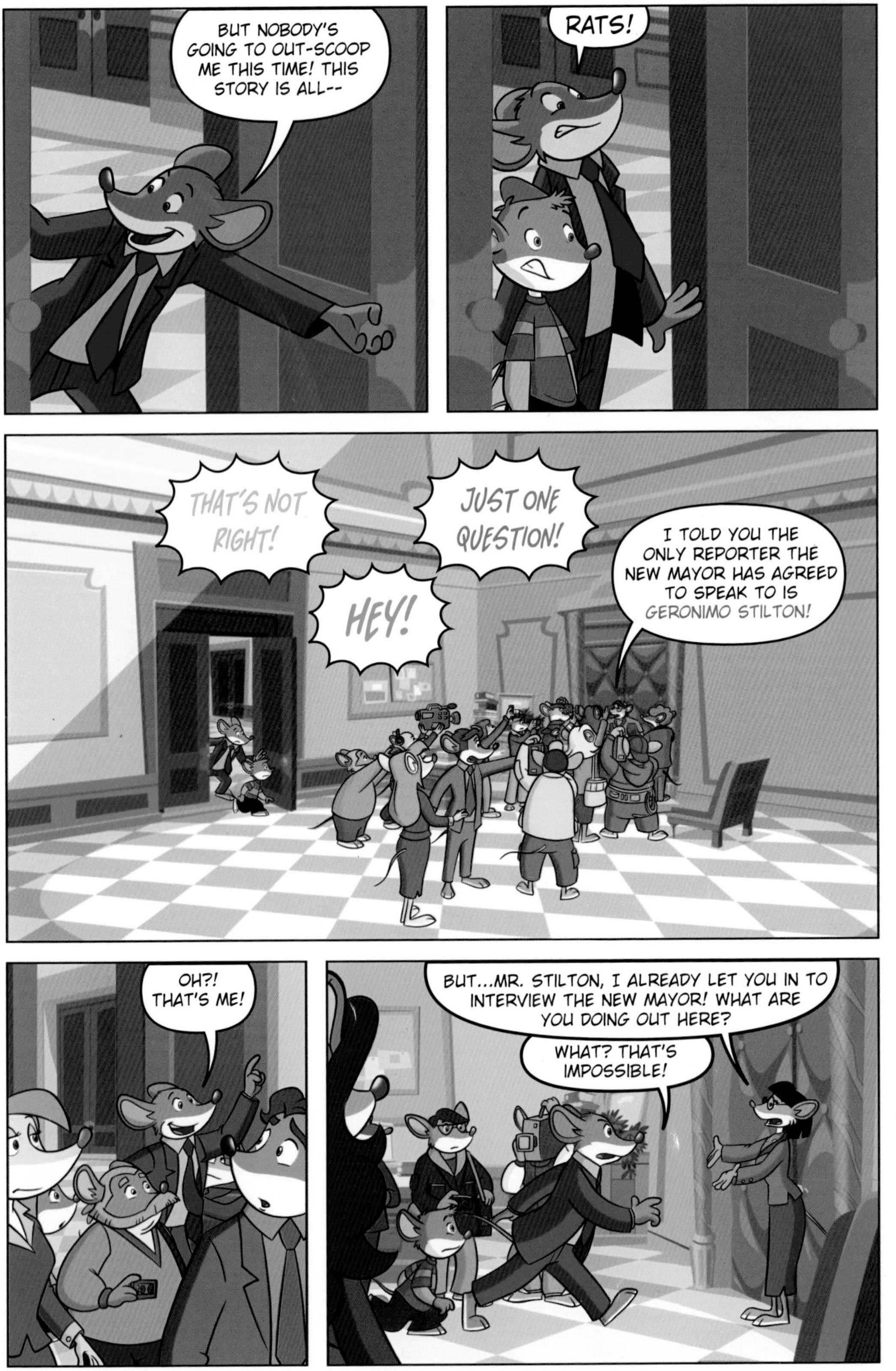
BUT NOBODY'S GOING TO OUT-SCOOP ME THIS TIME! THIS STORY IS ALL--
RATS!
THAT'S NOT RIGHT!
JUST ONE QUESTION!
HEY!
I TOLD YOU THE ONLY REPORTER THE NEW MAYOR HAS AGREED TO SPEAK TO IS GERONIMO STILTON!
OH?! THAT'S ME!
BUT...MR. STILTON, I ALREADY LET YOU IN TO INTERVIEW THE NEW MAYOR! WHAT ARE YOU DOING OUT HERE?
WHAT? THAT'S IMPOSSIBLE!

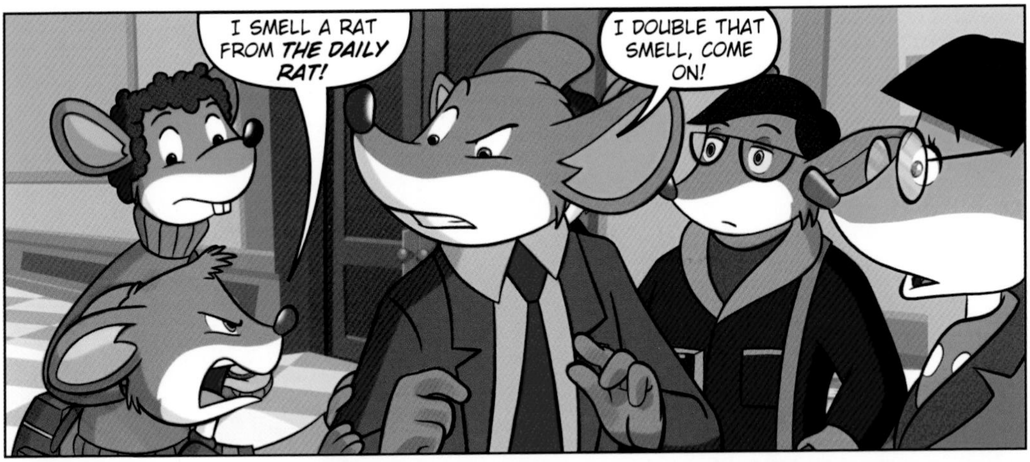
I SMELL A RAT FROM THE DAILY RAT!
I DOUBLE THAT SMELL, COME ON!

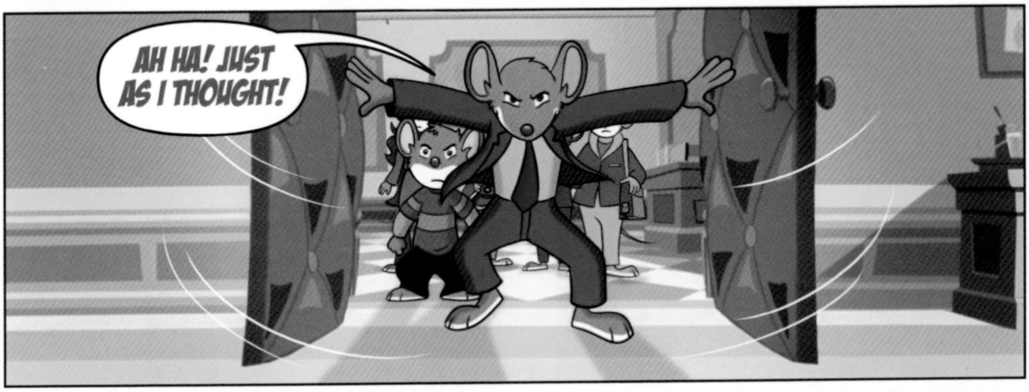
AH HA! JUST AS I THOUGHT!

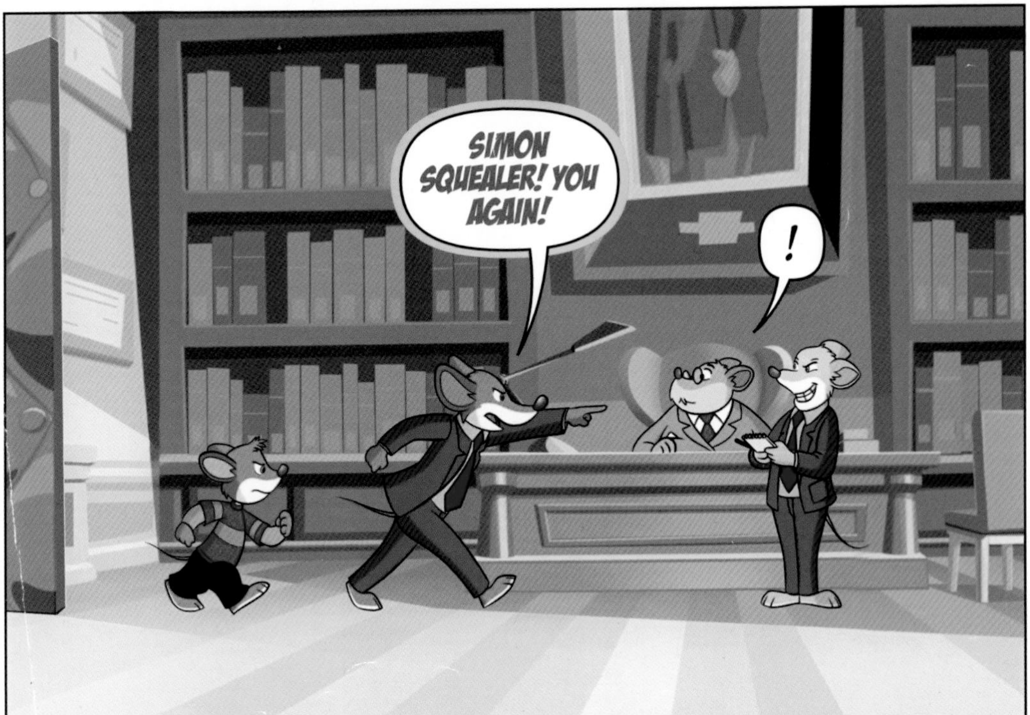
SIMON SQUEALER! YOU AGAIN!
!

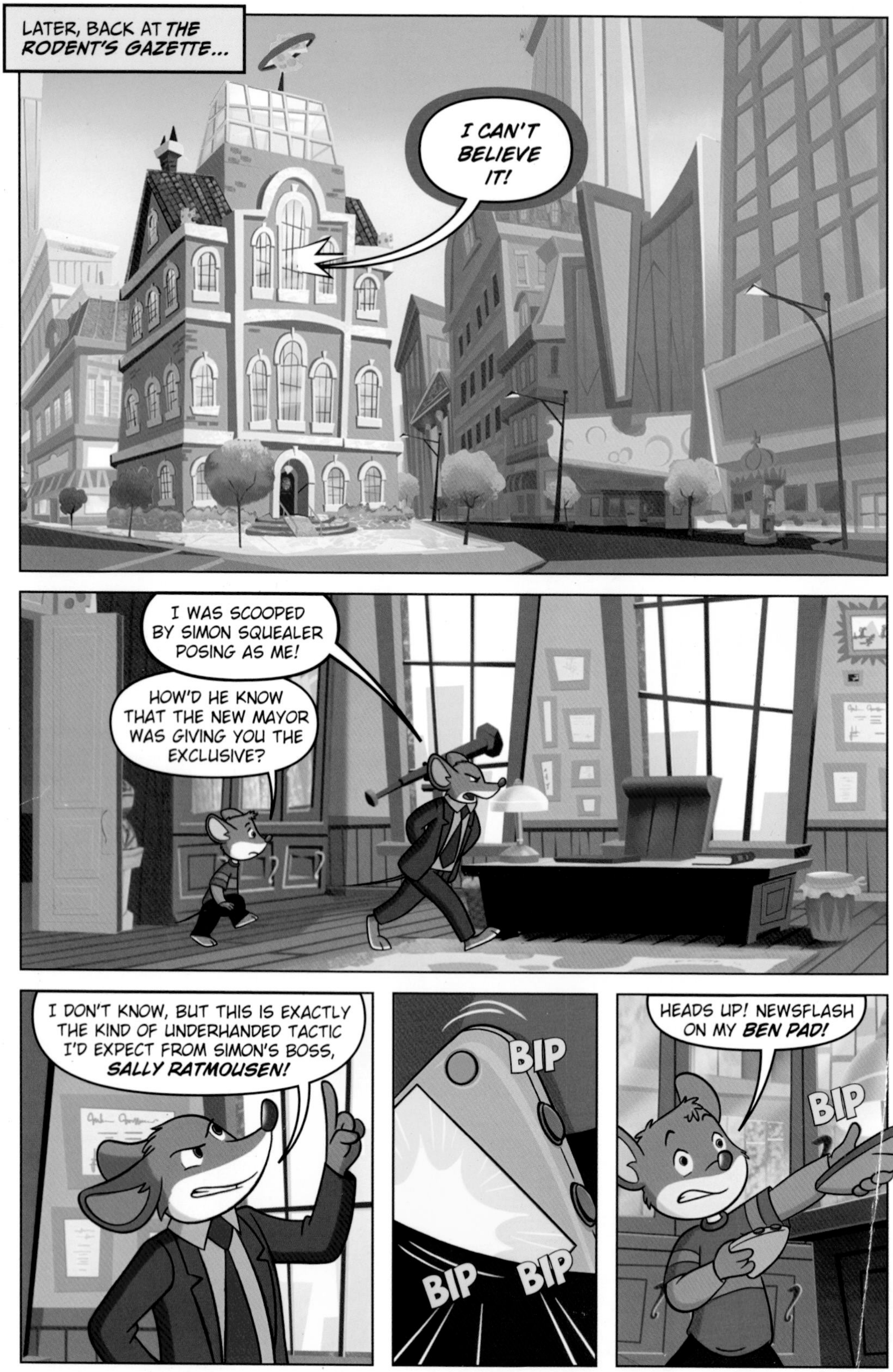
LATER, BACK AT *THE RODENT'S GAZETTE...*
I CAN'T BELIEVE IT!
I WAS SCOOPED BY SIMON SQUEALER POSING AS ME!
HOW'D HE KNOW THAT THE NEW MAYOR WAS GIVING YOU THE EXCLUSIVE?
I DON'T KNOW, BUT THIS IS EXACTLY THE KIND OF UNDERHANDED TACTIC I'D EXPECT FROM SIMON'S BOSS, ***SALLY RATMOUSEN!***
BIP
BIP
BIP
HEADS UP! NEWSFLASH ON MY ***BEN PAD!***
BIP

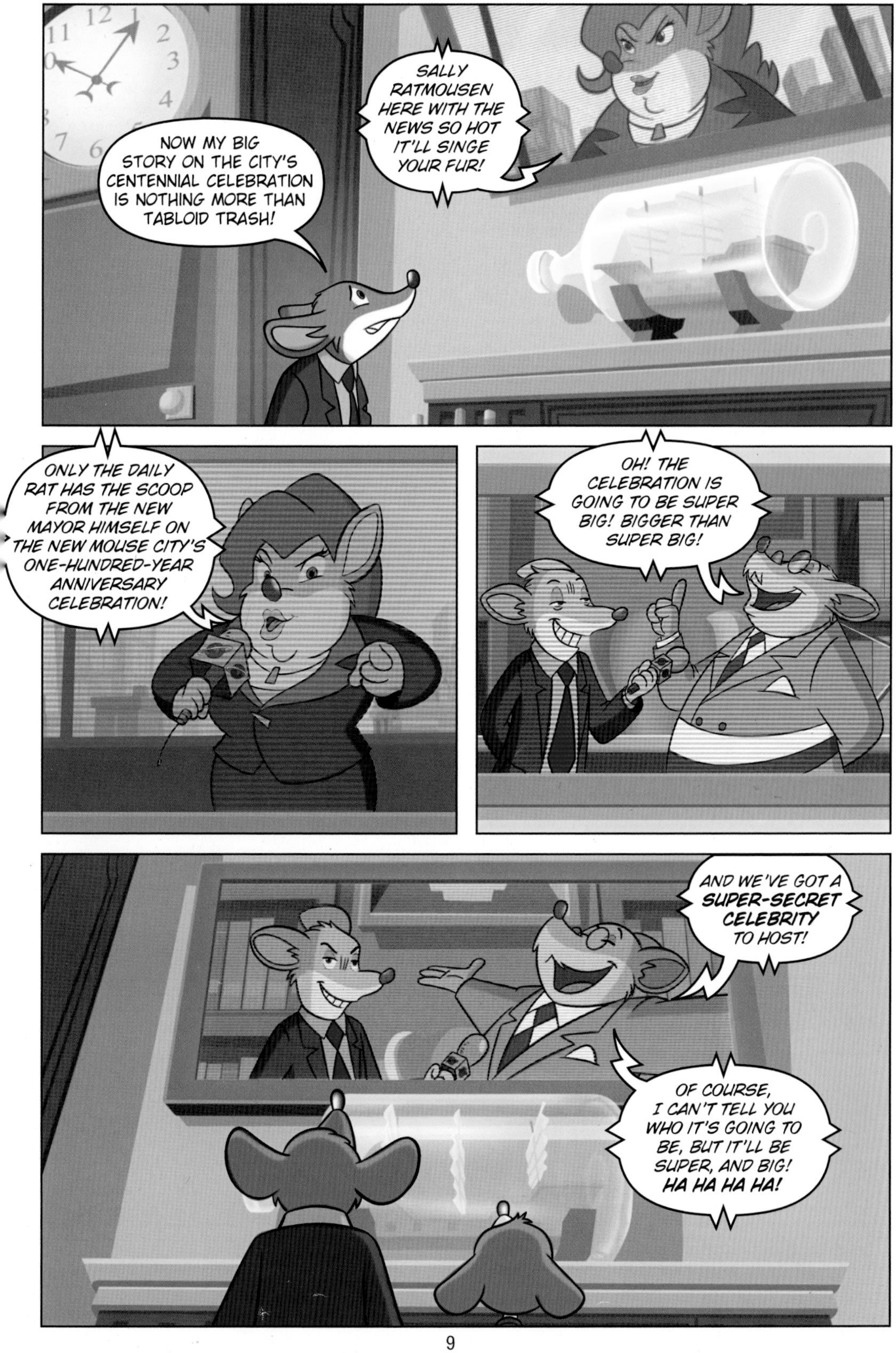
SALLY RATMOUSEN HERE WITH THE NEWS SO HOT IT'LL SINGE YOUR FUR!
NOW MY BIG STORY ON THE CITY'S CENTENNIAL CELEBRATION IS NOTHING MORE THAN TABLOID TRASH!
ONLY THE DAILY RAT HAS THE SCOOP FROM THE NEW MAYOR HIMSELF ON THE NEW MOUSE CITY'S ONE-HUNDRED-YEAR ANNIVERSARY CELEBRATION!
OH! THE CELEBRATION IS GOING TO BE SUPER BIG! BIGGER THAN SUPER BIG!
AND WE'VE GOT A **SUPER-SECRET CELEBRITY** TO HOST!
OF COURSE, I CAN'T TELL YOU WHO IT'S GOING TO BE, BUT IT'LL BE SUPER, AND BIG! **HA HA HA HA!**

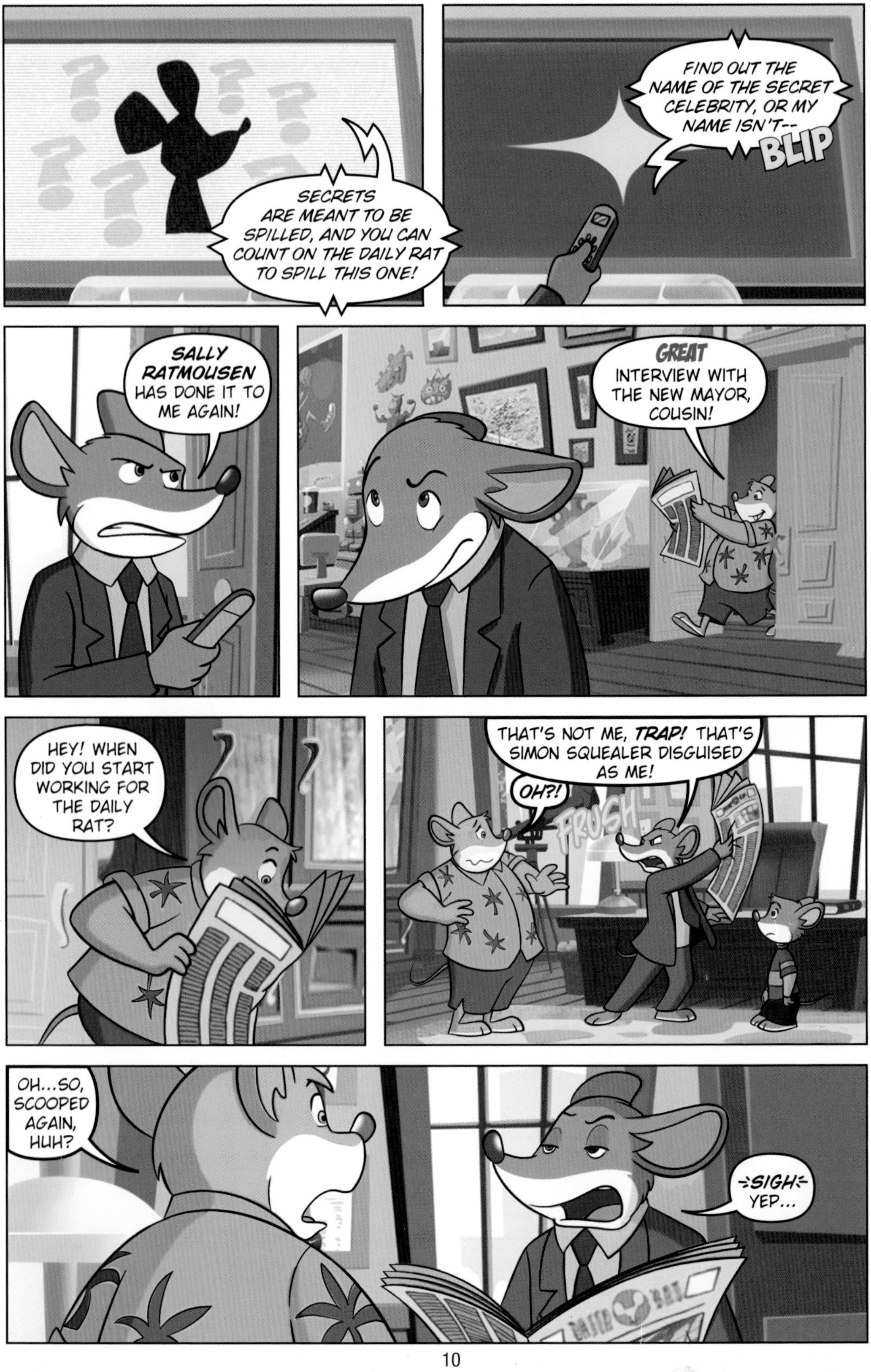
SECRETS ARE MEANT TO BE SPILLED, AND YOU CAN COUNT ON THE DAILY RAT TO SPILL THIS ONE!
FIND OUT THE NAME OF THE SECRET CELEBRITY, OR MY NAME ISN'T--
BLIP
SALLY RATMOUSEN HAS DONE IT TO ME AGAIN!
GREAT INTERVIEW WITH THE NEW MAYOR, COUSIN!
HEY! WHEN DID YOU START WORKING FOR THE DAILY RAT?
THAT'S NOT ME, TRAP! THAT'S SIMON SQUEALER DISGUISED AS ME!
OH?!
FRUSH
OH...SO, SCOOPED AGAIN, HUH?
SIGH YEP...

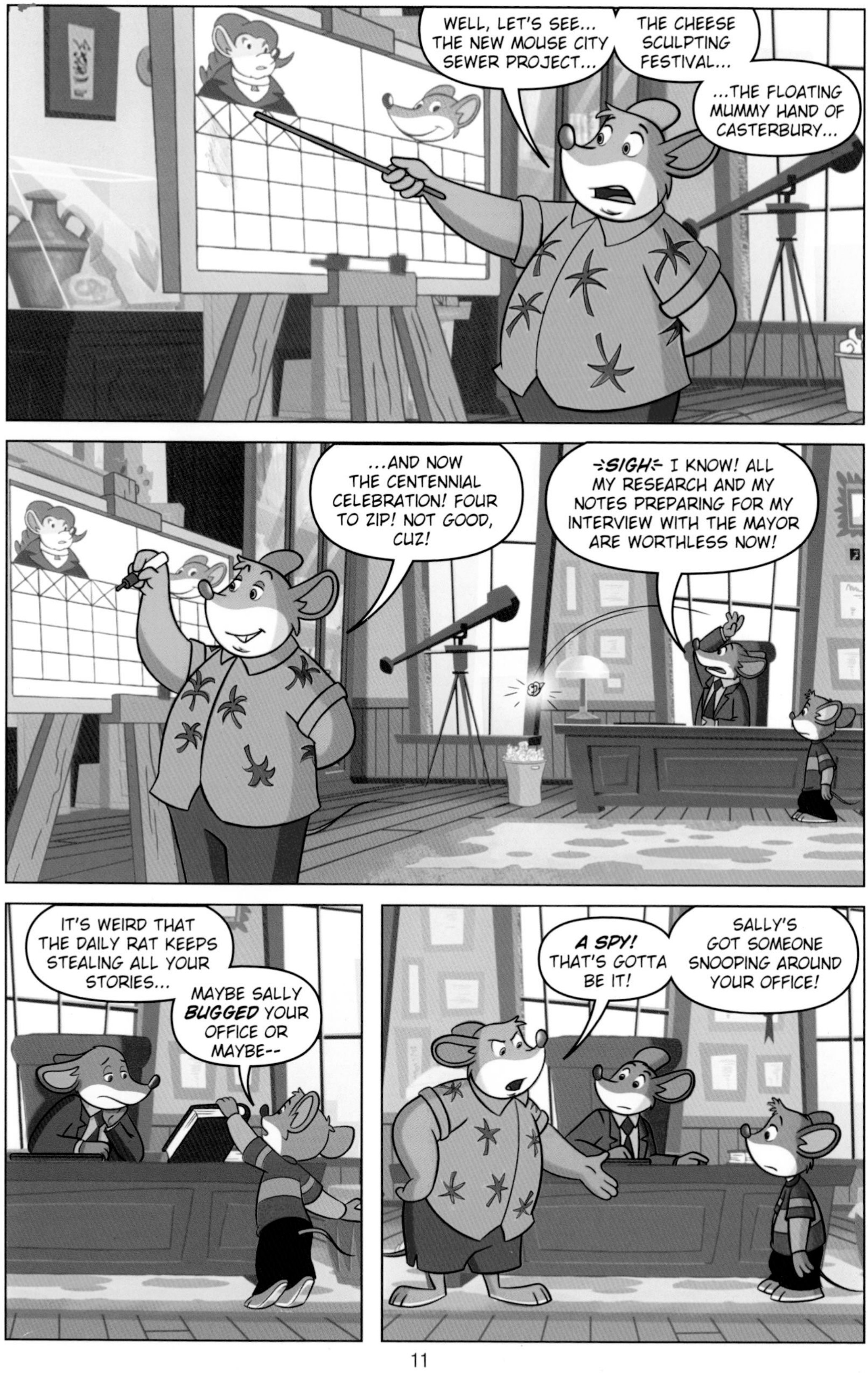
WELL, LET'S SEE... THE NEW MOUSE CITY SEWER PROJECT...
THE CHEESE SCULPTING FESTIVAL...
...THE FLOATING MUMMY HAND OF CASTERBURY...
...AND NOW THE CENTENNIAL CELEBRATION! FOUR TO ZIP! NOT GOOD, CUZ!
SIGH I KNOW! ALL MY RESEARCH AND MY NOTES PREPARING FOR MY INTERVIEW WITH THE MAYOR ARE WORTHLESS NOW!
IT'S WEIRD THAT THE DAILY RAT KEEPS STEALING ALL YOUR STORIES...
MAYBE SALLY **BUGGED** YOUR OFFICE OR MAYBE--
A SPY! THAT'S GOTTA BE IT!
SALLY'S GOT SOMEONE SNOOPING AROUND YOUR OFFICE!

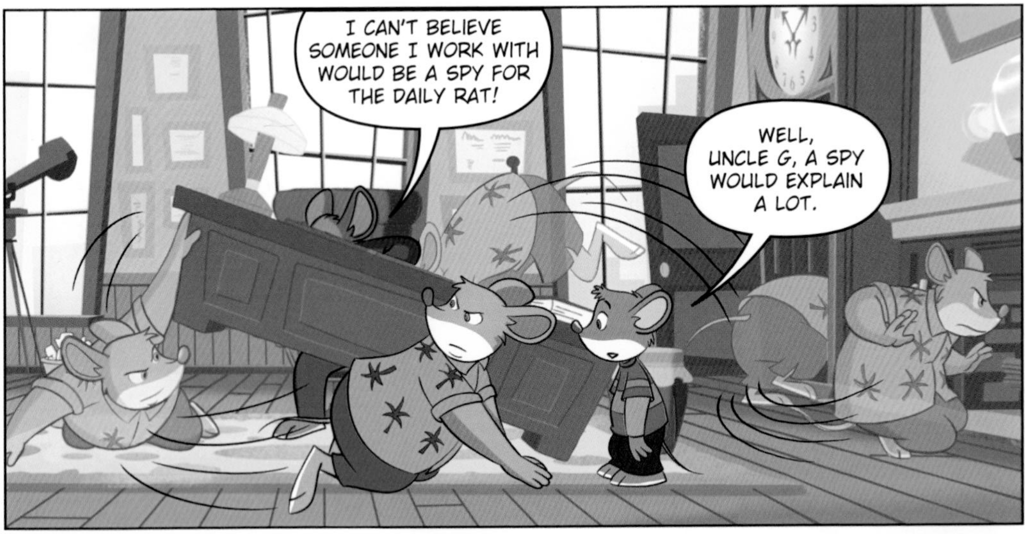
I CAN'T BELIEVE SOMEONE I WORK WITH WOULD BE A SPY FOR THE DAILY RAT!
WELL, UNCLE G, A SPY WOULD EXPLAIN A LOT.

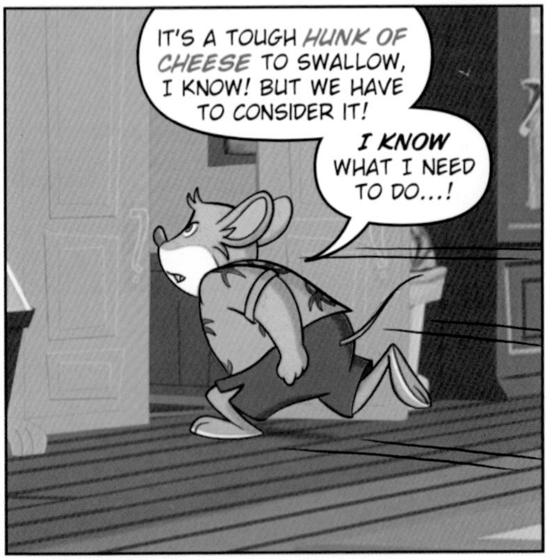
IT'S A TOUGH HUNK OF CHEESE TO SWALLOW, I KNOW! BUT WE HAVE TO CONSIDER IT!
I KNOW WHAT I NEED TO DO...!

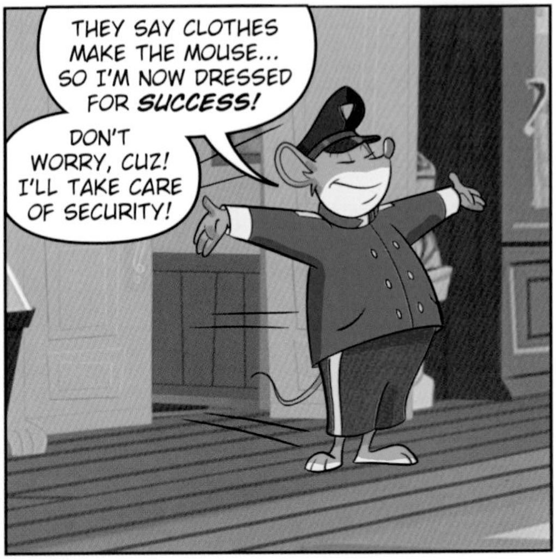
THEY SAY CLOTHES MAKE THE MOUSE... SO I'M NOW DRESSED FOR SUCCESS!
DON'T WORRY, CUZ! I'LL TAKE CARE OF SECURITY!

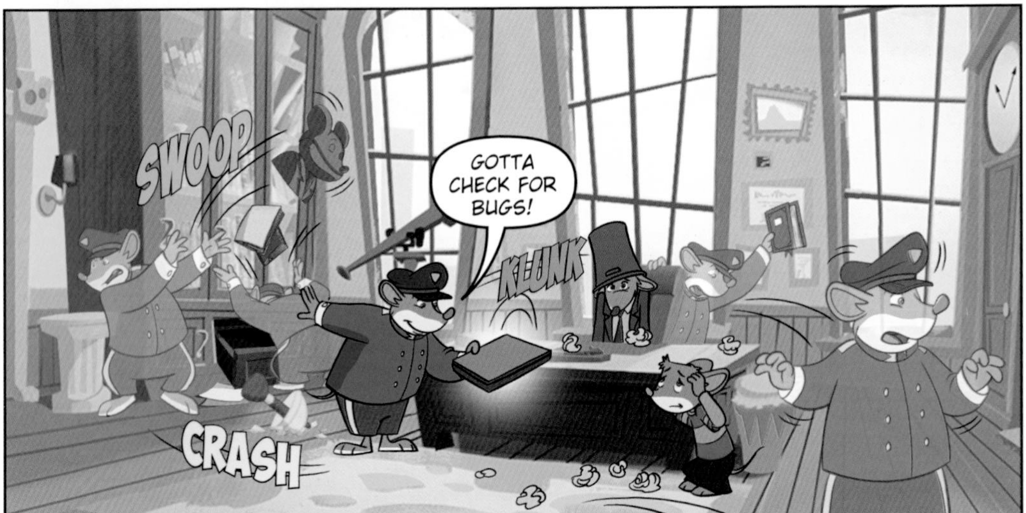
SWOOP
GOTTA CHECK FOR BUGS!
KLUNK
CRASH

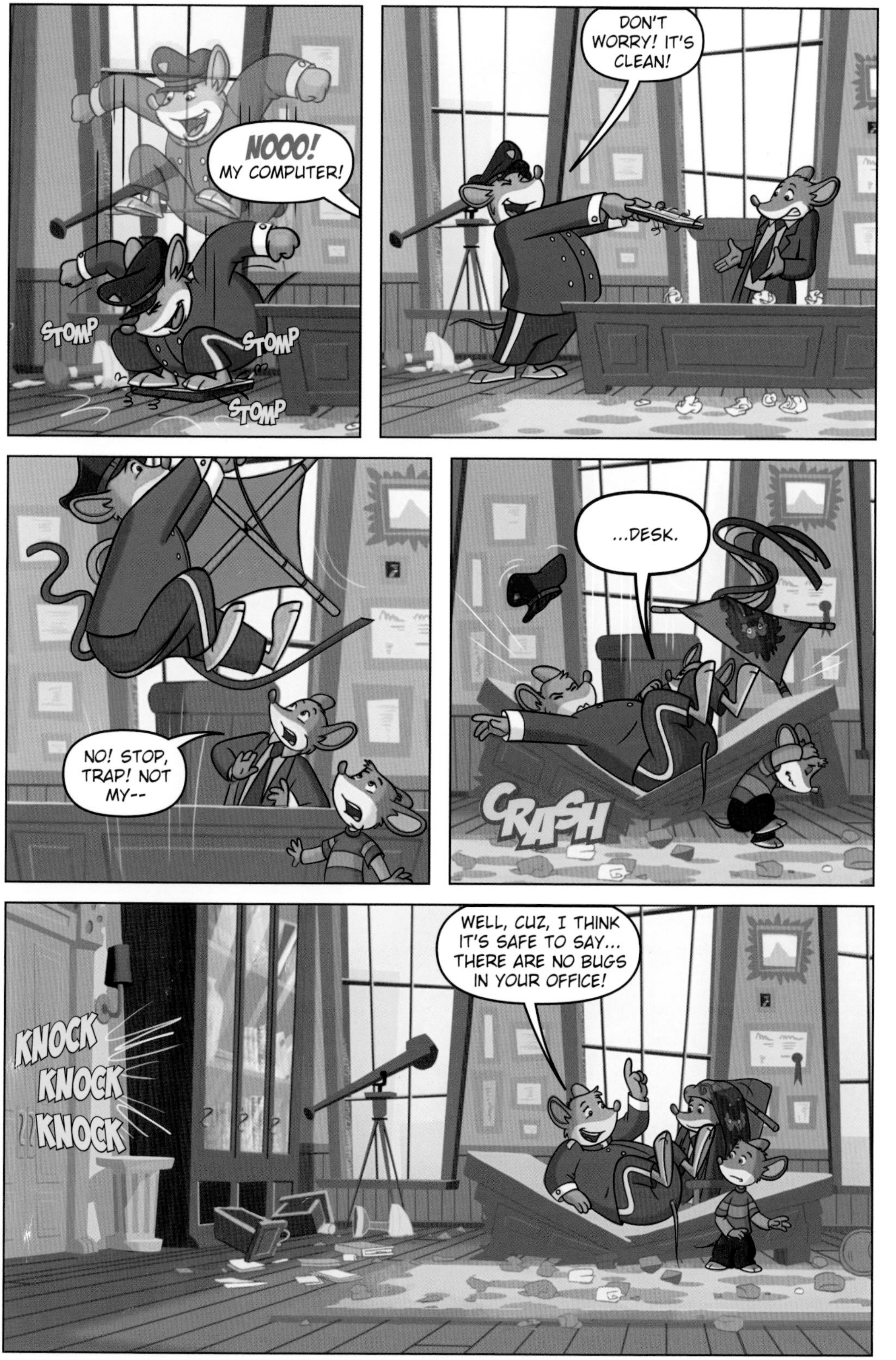
NOOO! MY COMPUTER!
STOMP
STOMP
STOMP
DON'T WORRY! IT'S CLEAN!
NO! STOP, TRAP! NOT MY--
...DESK.
CRASH
KNOCK
KNOCK
KNOCK
WELL, CUZ, I THINK IT'S SAFE TO SAY... THERE ARE NO BUGS IN YOUR OFFICE!

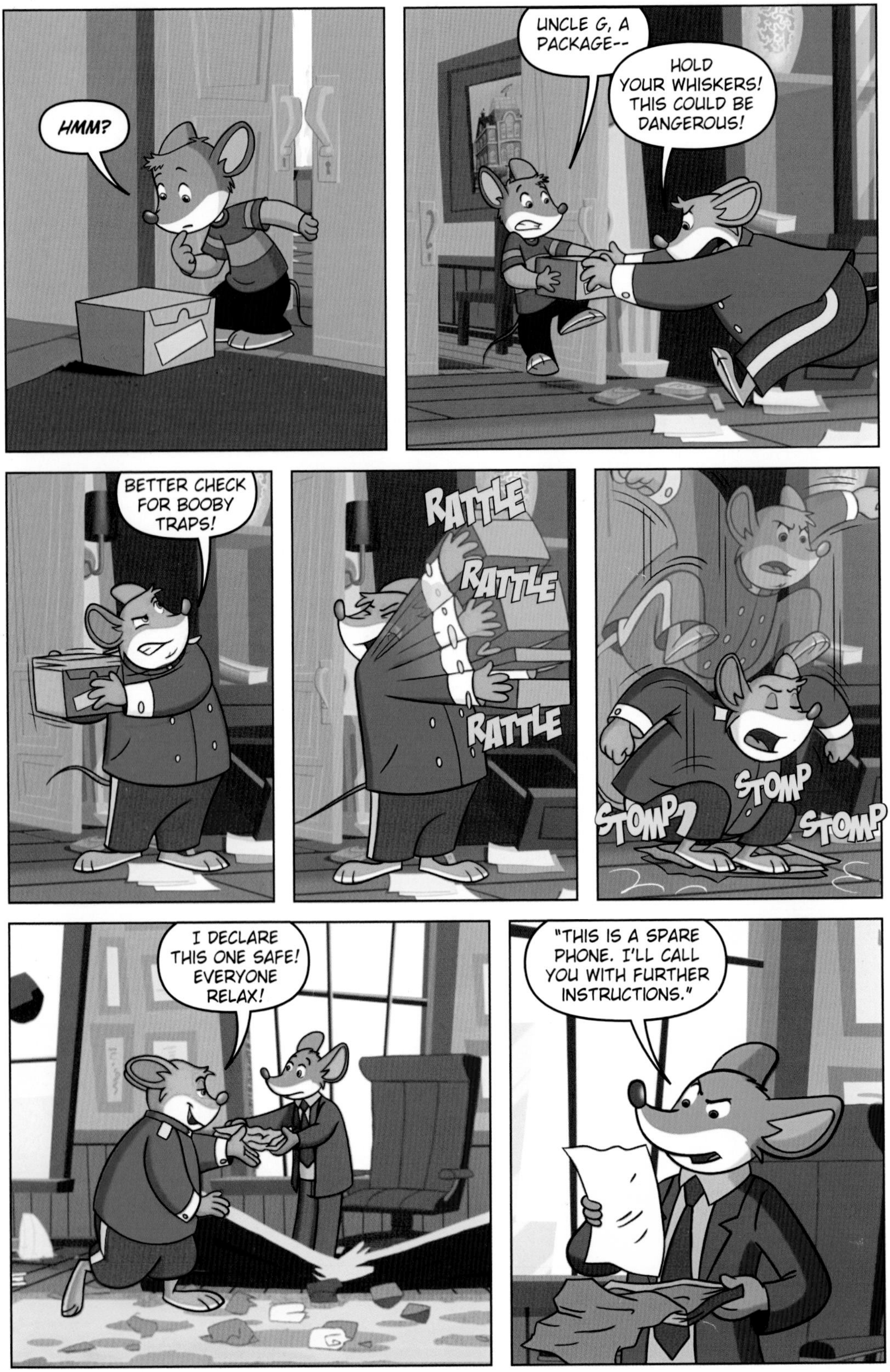
HMM?
UNCLE G, A PACKAGE--
HOLD YOUR WHISKERS! THIS COULD BE DANGEROUS!
BETTER CHECK FOR BOOBY TRAPS!
RATTLE
RATTLE
RATTLE
STOMP
STOMP
STOMP
I DECLARE THIS ONE SAFE! EVERYONE RELAX!
"THIS IS A SPARE PHONE. I'LL CALL YOU WITH FURTHER INSTRUCTIONS."

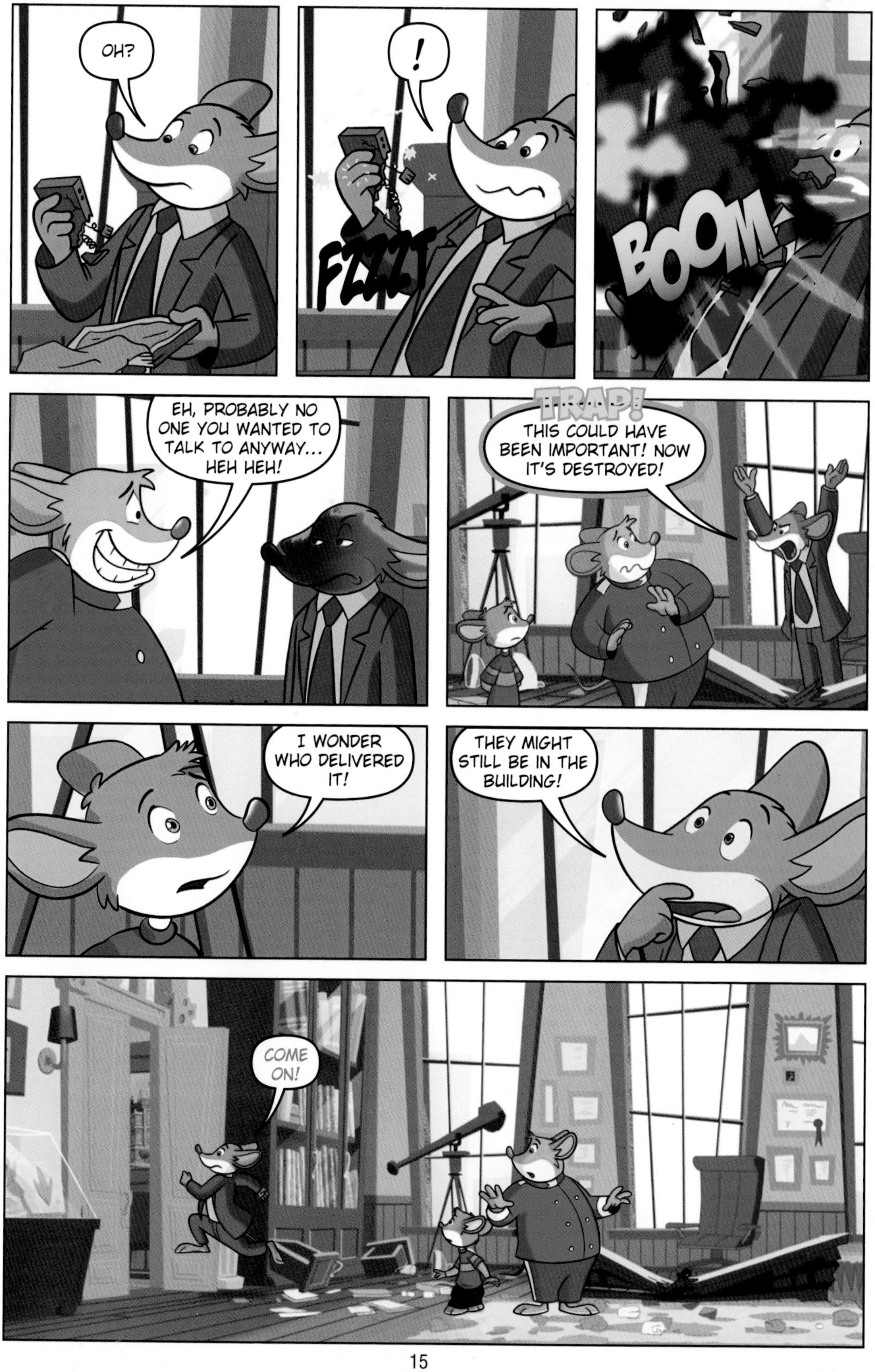
OH?
!
FZZZT
BOOM!
EH, PROBABLY NO ONE YOU WANTED TO TALK TO ANYWAY... HEH HEH!
TRAP!
THIS COULD HAVE BEEN IMPORTANT! NOW IT'S DESTROYED!
I WONDER WHO DELIVERED IT!
THEY MIGHT STILL BE IN THE BUILDING!
COME ON!

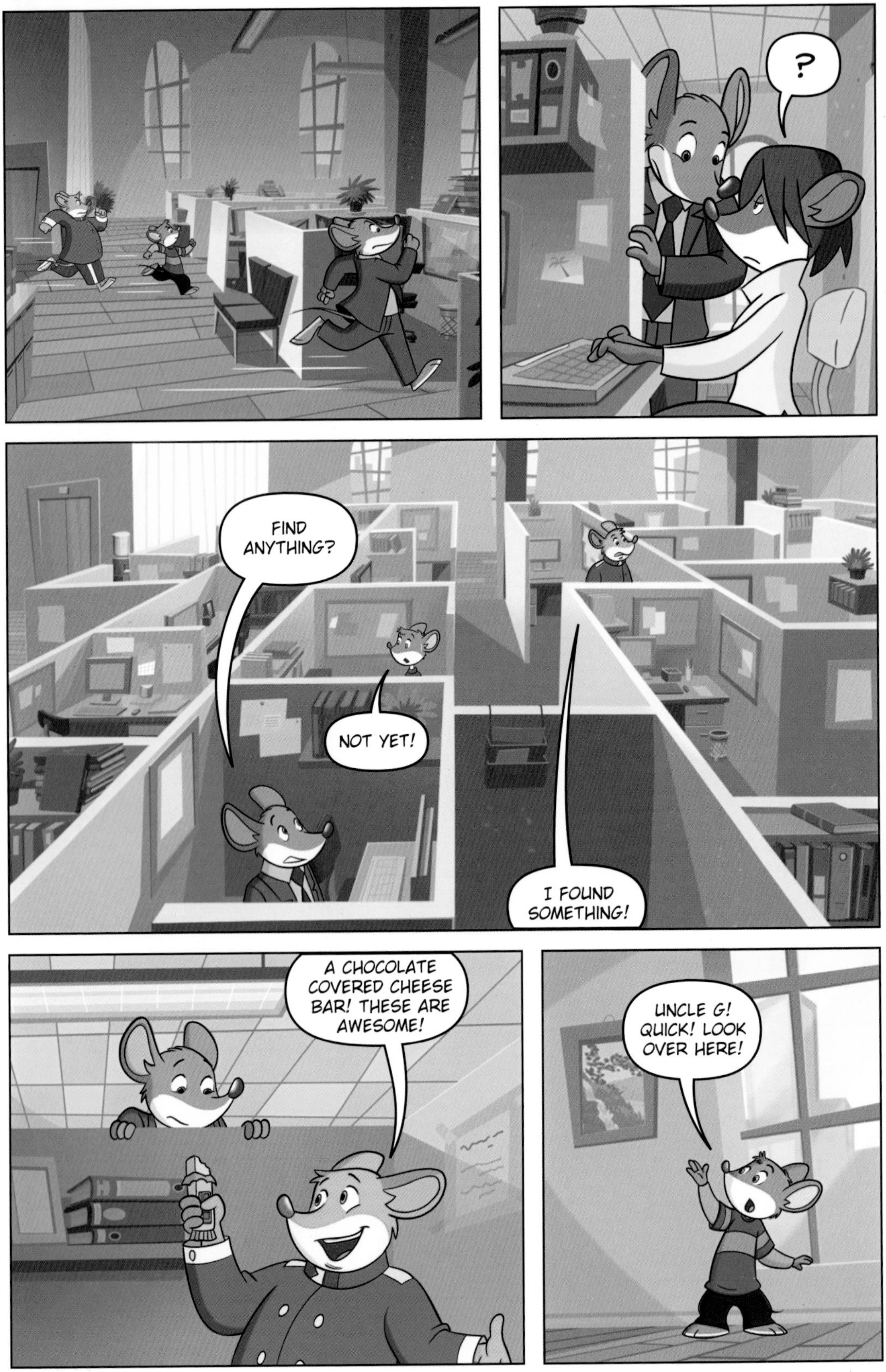
?
FIND ANYTHING?
NOT YET!
I FOUND SOMETHING!
A CHOCOLATE COVERED CHEESE BAR! THESE ARE AWESOME!
UNCLE G! QUICK! LOOK OVER HERE!

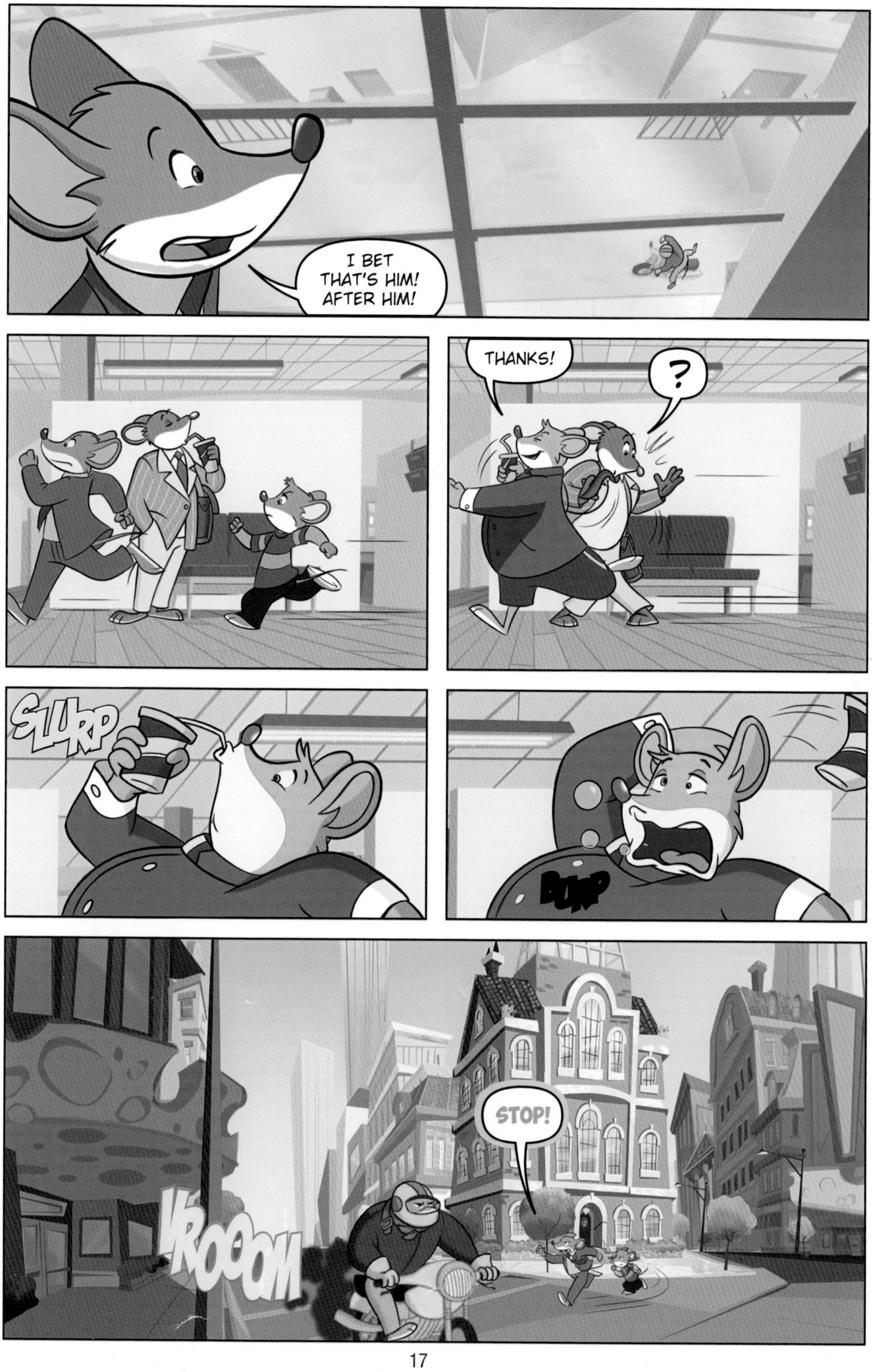
I BET THAT'S HIM! AFTER HIM!
THANKS!
?
SLURP
BUMP
STOP!
VROOOM

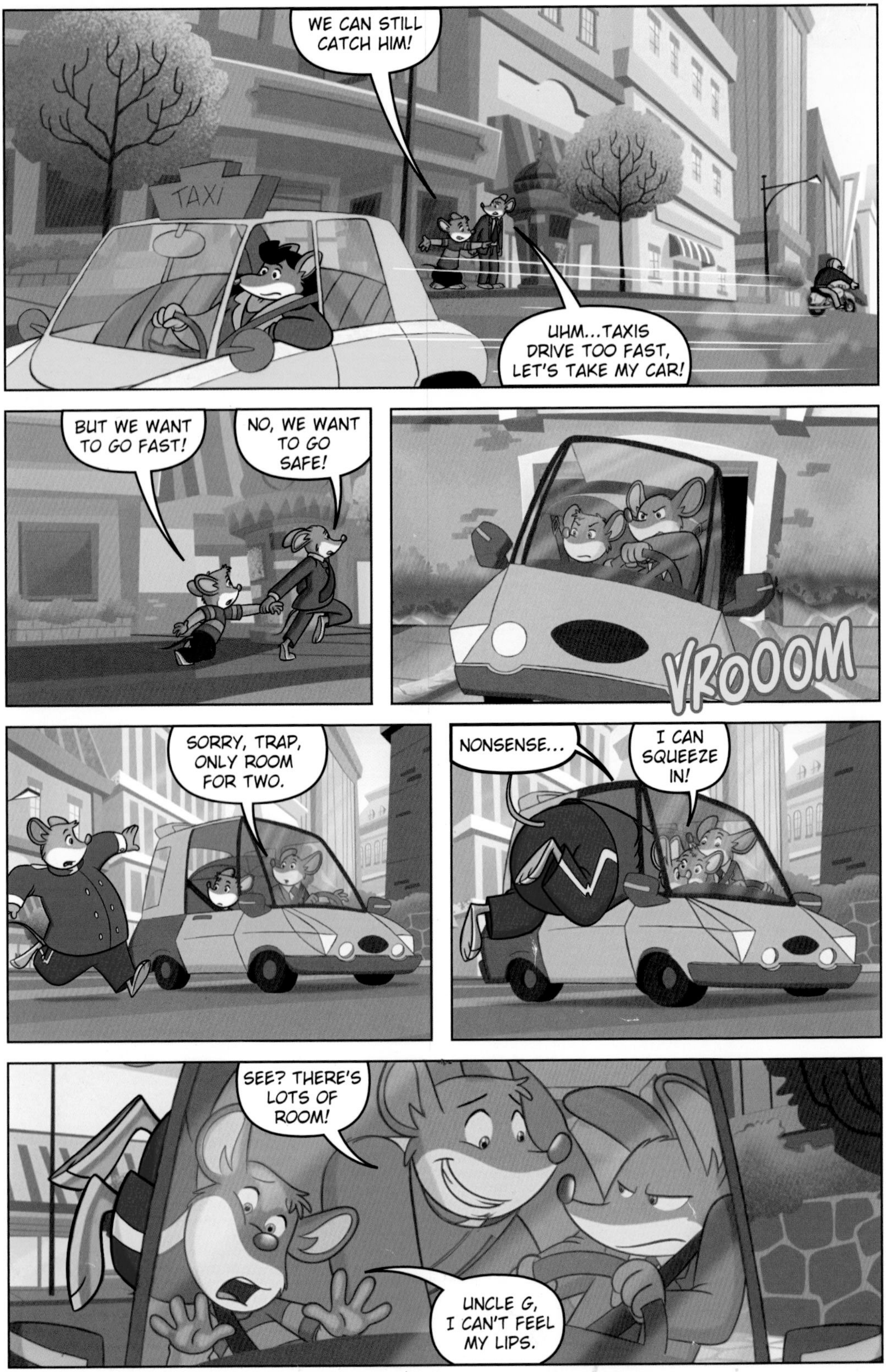

TAXI
WE CAN STILL CATCH HIM!
UHM...TAXIS DRIVE TOO FAST, LET'S TAKE MY CAR!
BUT WE WANT TO GO FAST!
NO, WE WANT TO GO SAFE!
VROOOM
SORRY, TRAP, ONLY ROOM FOR TWO.
NONSENSE...
I CAN SQUEEZE IN!
SEE? THERE'S LOTS OF ROOM!
UNCLE G, I CAN'T FEEL MY LIPS.

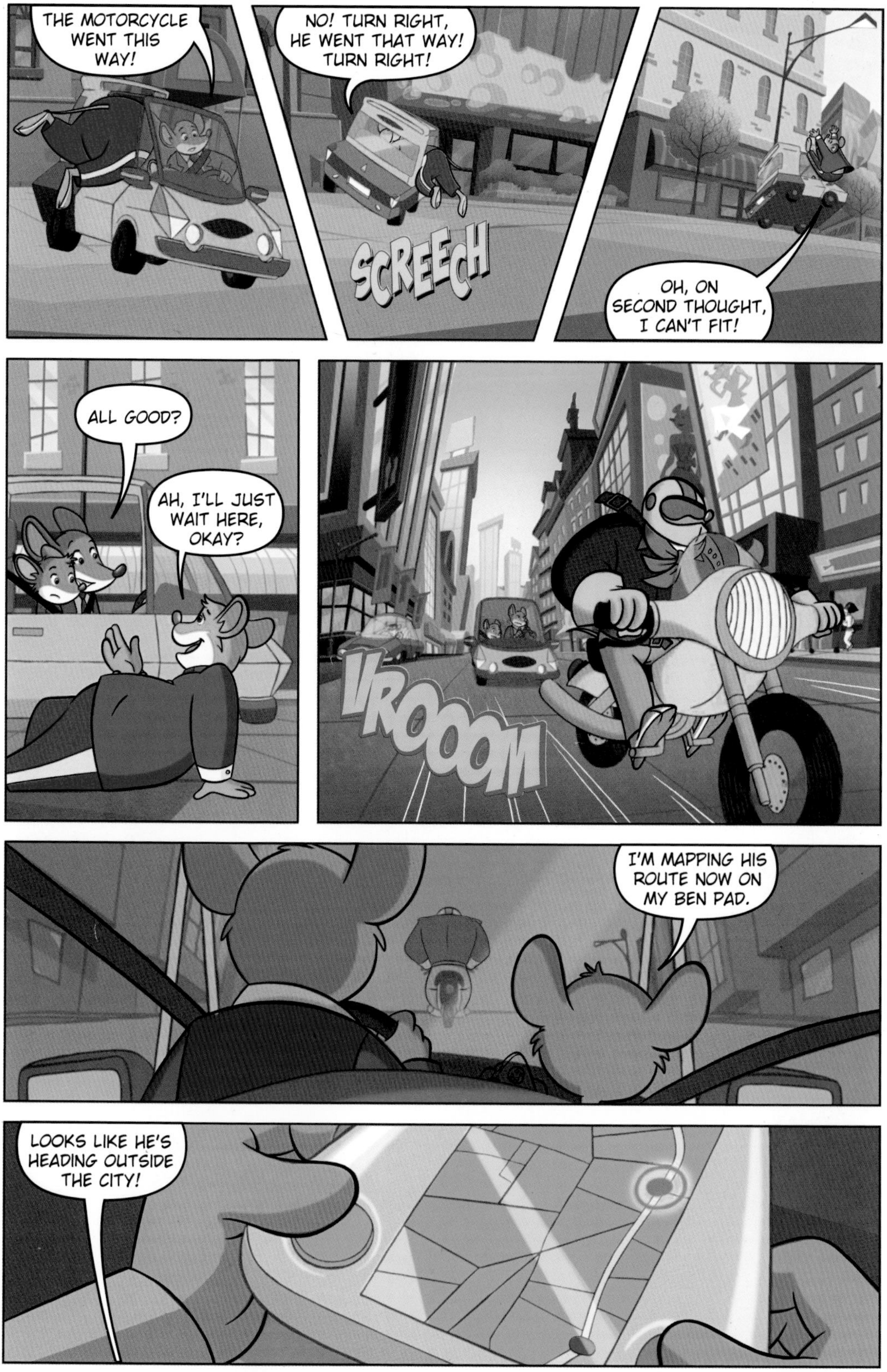

THE MOTORCYCLE WENT THIS WAY!
NO! TURN RIGHT, HE WENT THAT WAY! TURN RIGHT!
SCREECH
OH, ON SECOND THOUGHT, I CAN'T FIT!
ALL GOOD?
AH, I'LL JUST WAIT HERE, OKAY?
VROOOM
I'M MAPPING HIS ROUTE NOW ON MY BEN PAD.
LOOKS LIKE HE'S HEADING OUTSIDE THE CITY!

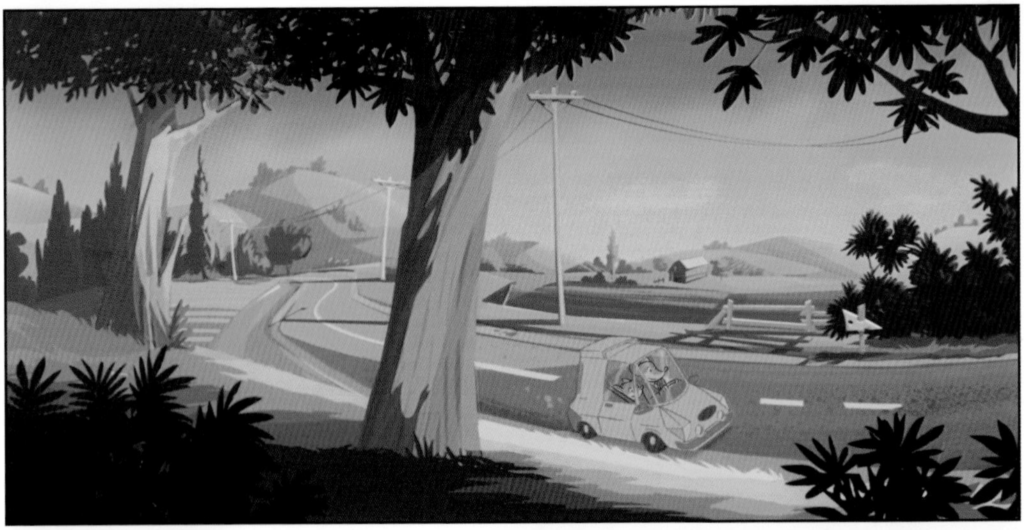

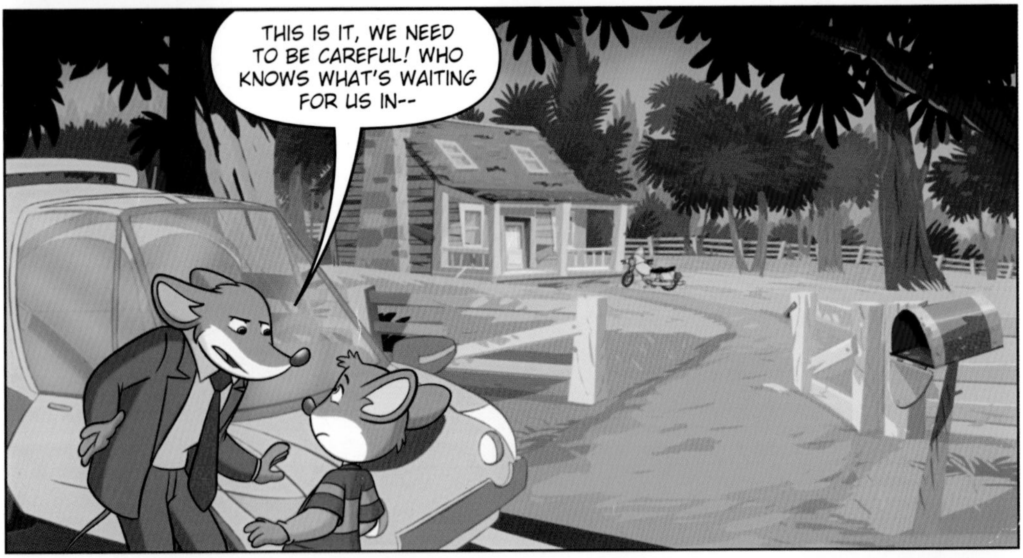
THIS IS IT, WE NEED TO BE CAREFUL! WHO KNOWS WHAT'S WAITING FOR US IN--

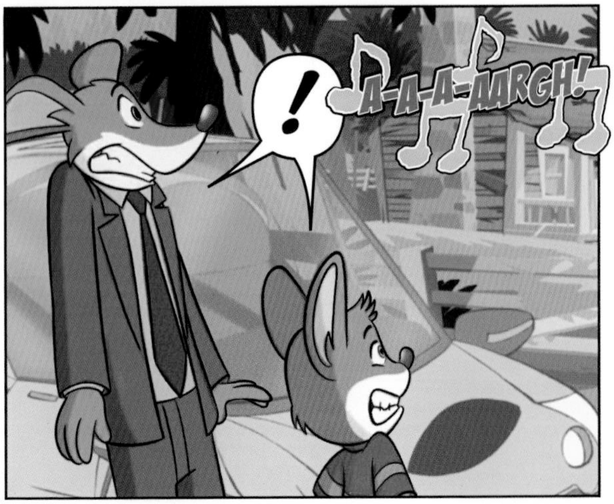
!
A-A-A-AARGH!

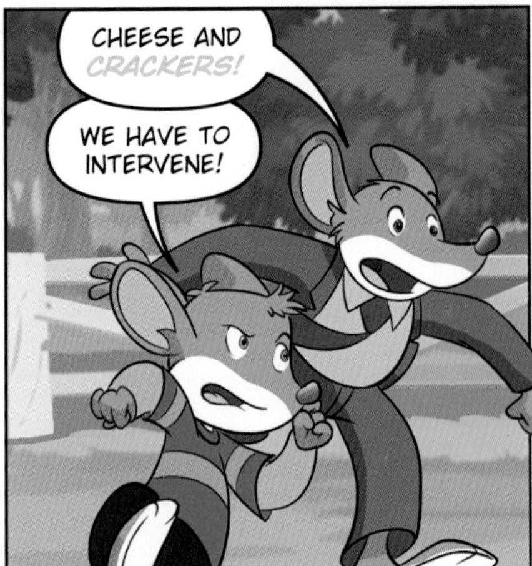
CHEESE AND CRACKERS!
WE HAVE TO INTERVENE!

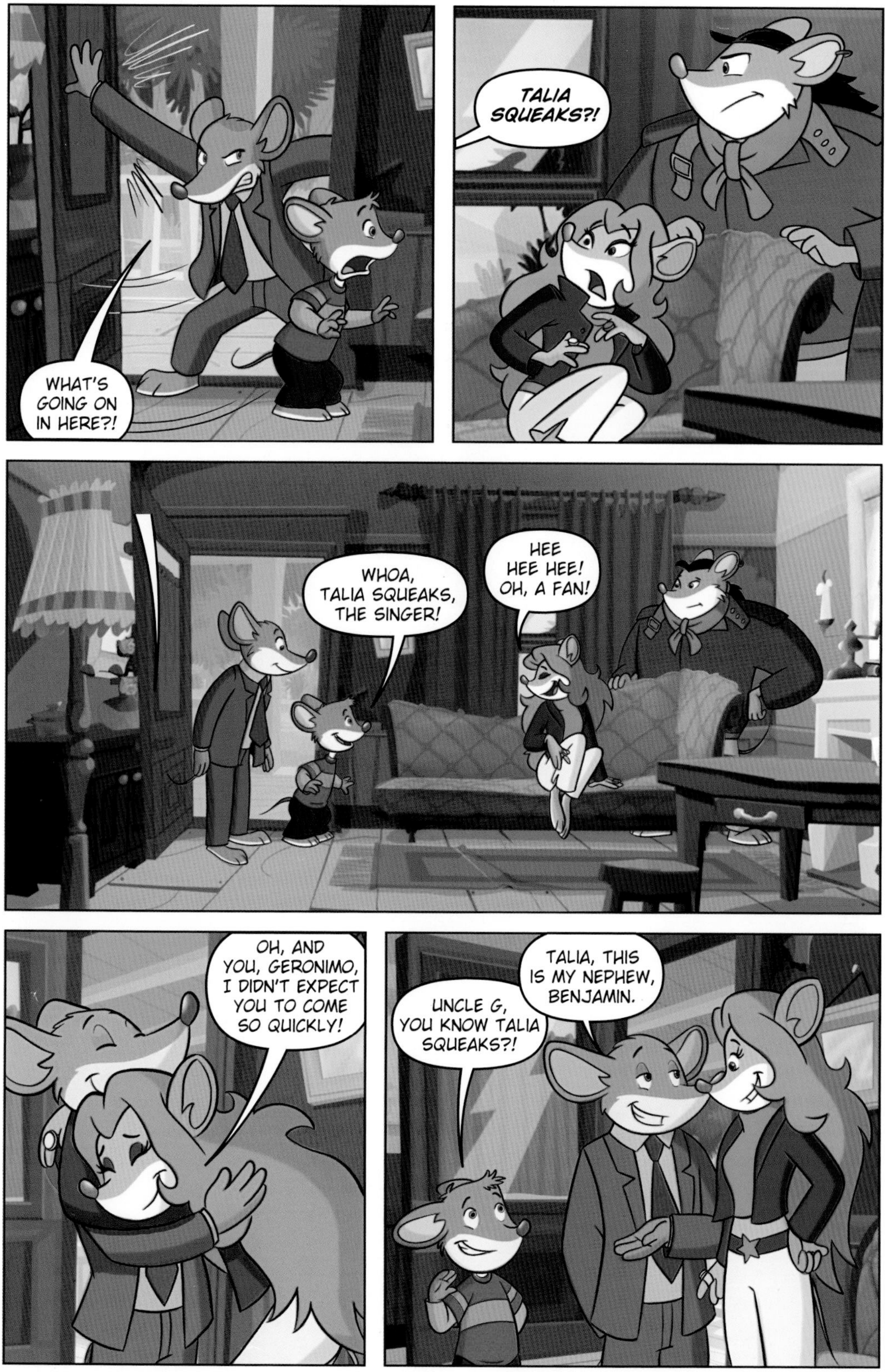
WHAT'S GOING ON IN HERE?!
TALIA SQUEAKS?!
WHOA, TALIA SQUEAKS, THE SINGER!
HEE HEE HEE! OH, A FAN!
OH, AND YOU, GERONIMO, I DIDN'T EXPECT YOU TO COME SO QUICKLY!
TALIA, THIS IS MY NEPHEW, BENJAMIN.
UNCLE G, YOU KNOW TALIA SQUEAKS?!

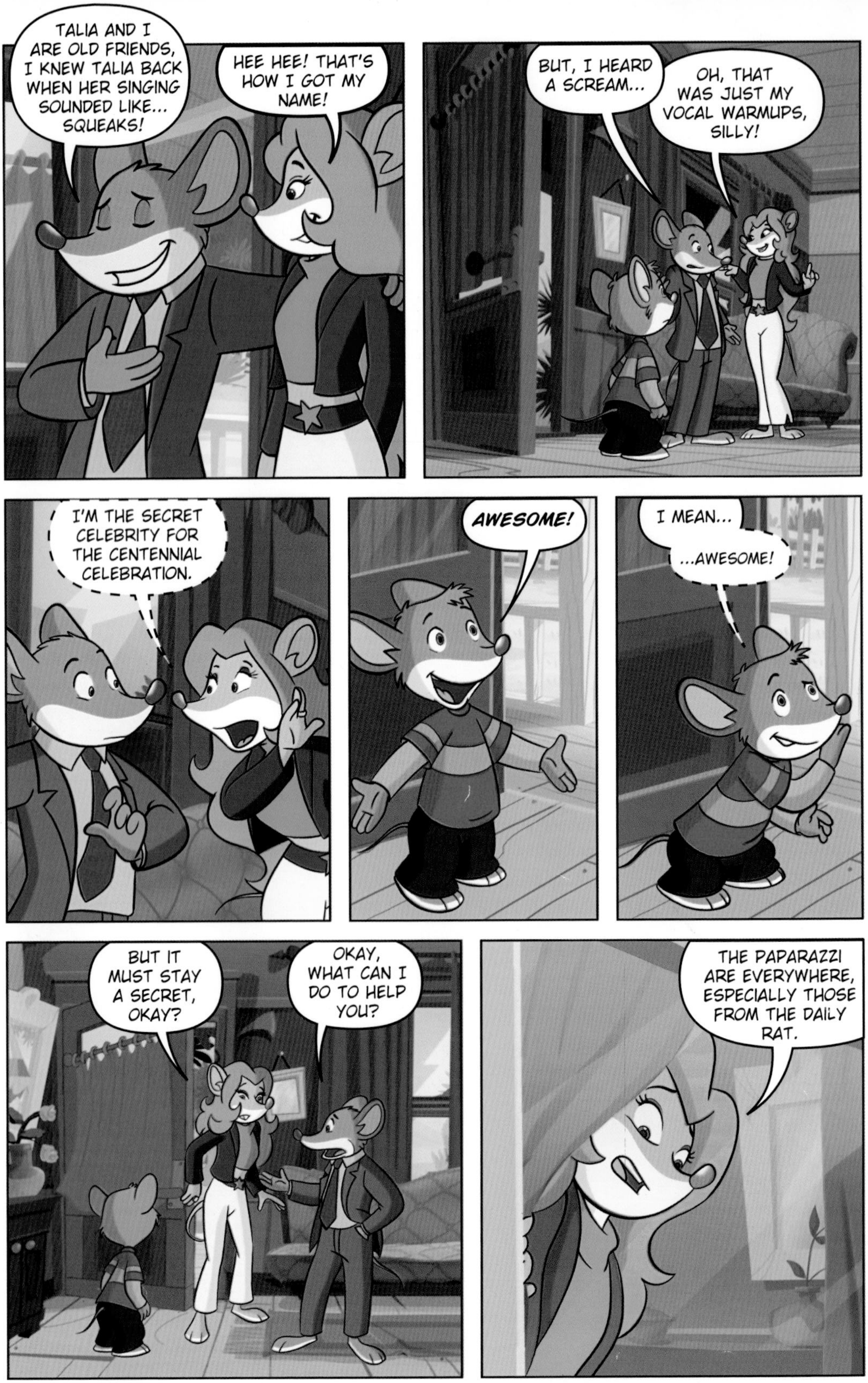
TALIA AND I ARE OLD FRIENDS, I KNEW TALIA BACK WHEN HER SINGING SOUNDED LIKE... SQUEAKS!
HEE HEE! THAT'S HOW I GOT MY NAME!
BUT, I HEARD A SCREAM...
OH, THAT WAS JUST MY VOCAL WARMUPS, SILLY!
I'M THE SECRET CELEBRITY FOR THE CENTENNIAL CELEBRATION.
AWESOME!
I MEAN...
...AWESOME!
BUT IT MUST STAY A SECRET, OKAY?
OKAY, WHAT CAN I DO TO HELP YOU?
THE PAPARAZZI ARE EVERYWHERE, ESPECIALLY THOSE FROM THE DAILY RAT.

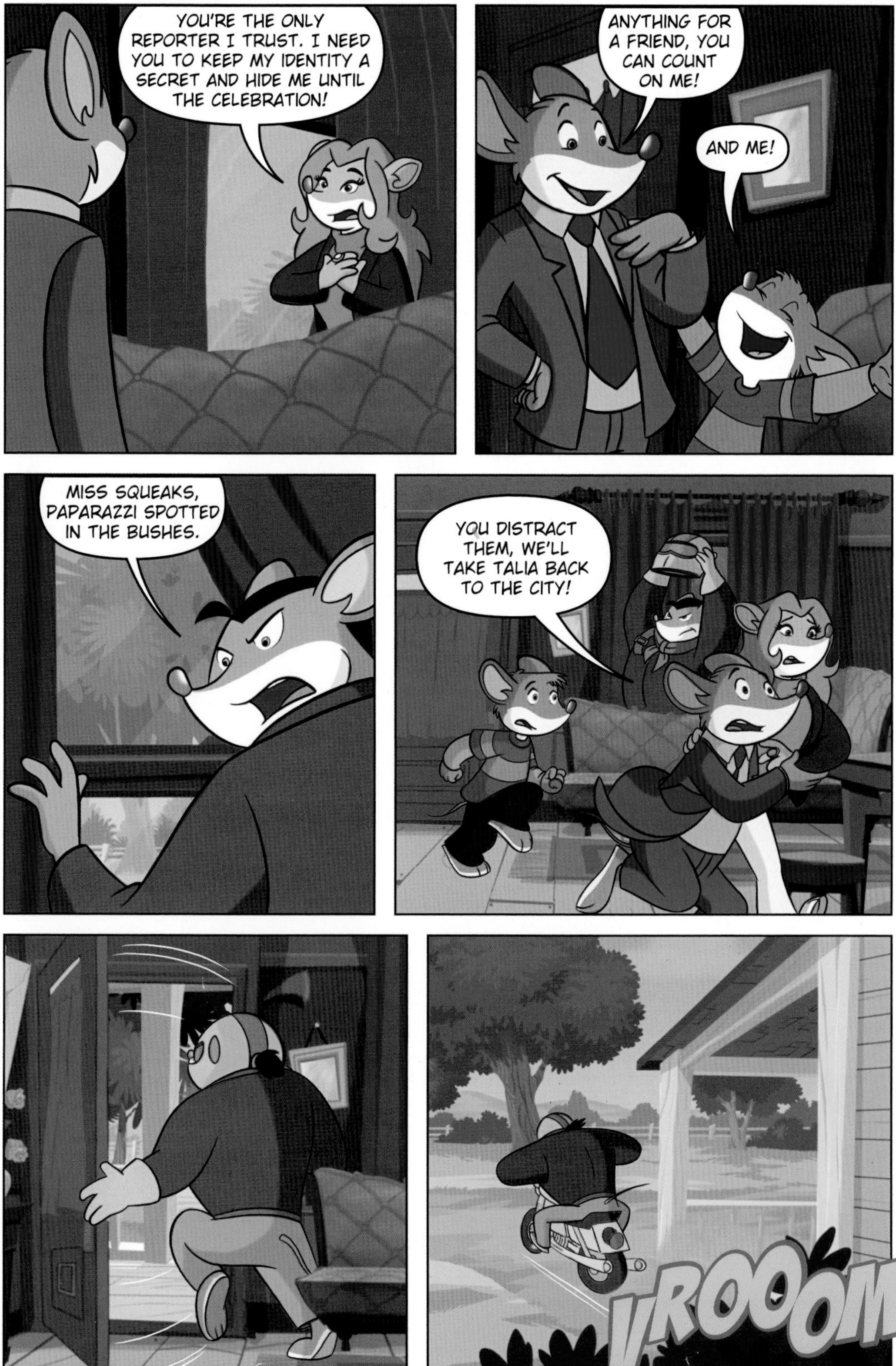
YOU'RE THE ONLY REPORTER I TRUST. I NEED YOU TO KEEP MY IDENTITY A SECRET AND HIDE ME UNTIL THE CELEBRATION!
ANYTHING FOR A FRIEND, YOU CAN COUNT ON ME!
AND ME!
MISS SQUEAKS, PAPARAZZI SPOTTED IN THE BUSHES.
YOU DISTRACT THEM, WE'LL TAKE TALIA BACK TO THE CITY!
VROOOM

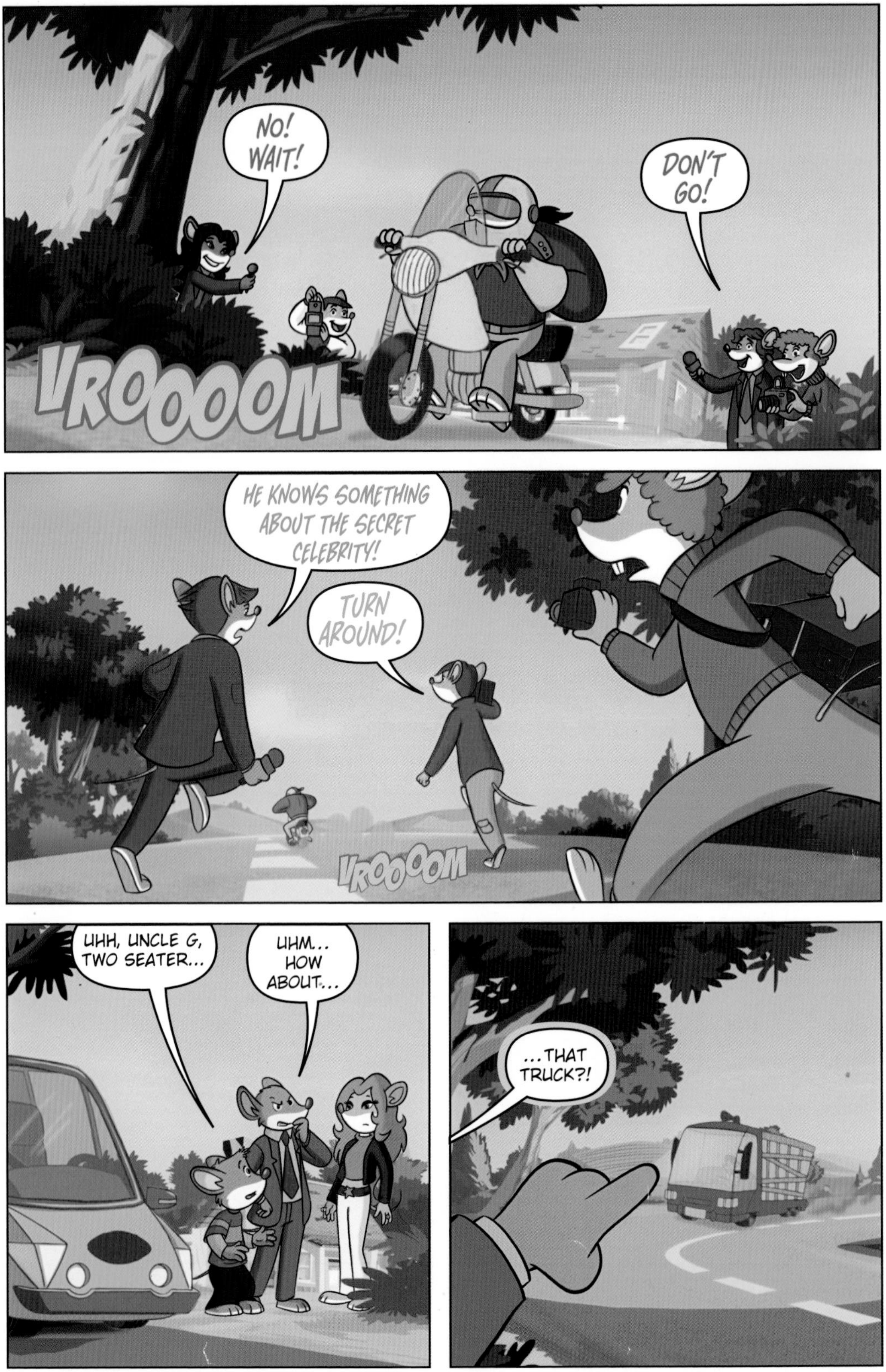
NO! WAIT!
DON'T GO!
VROOOOM
HE KNOWS SOMETHING ABOUT THE SECRET CELEBRITY!
TURN AROUND!
VROOOOM
UHH, UNCLE G, TWO SEATER...
UHM... HOW ABOUT...
...THAT TRUCK?!

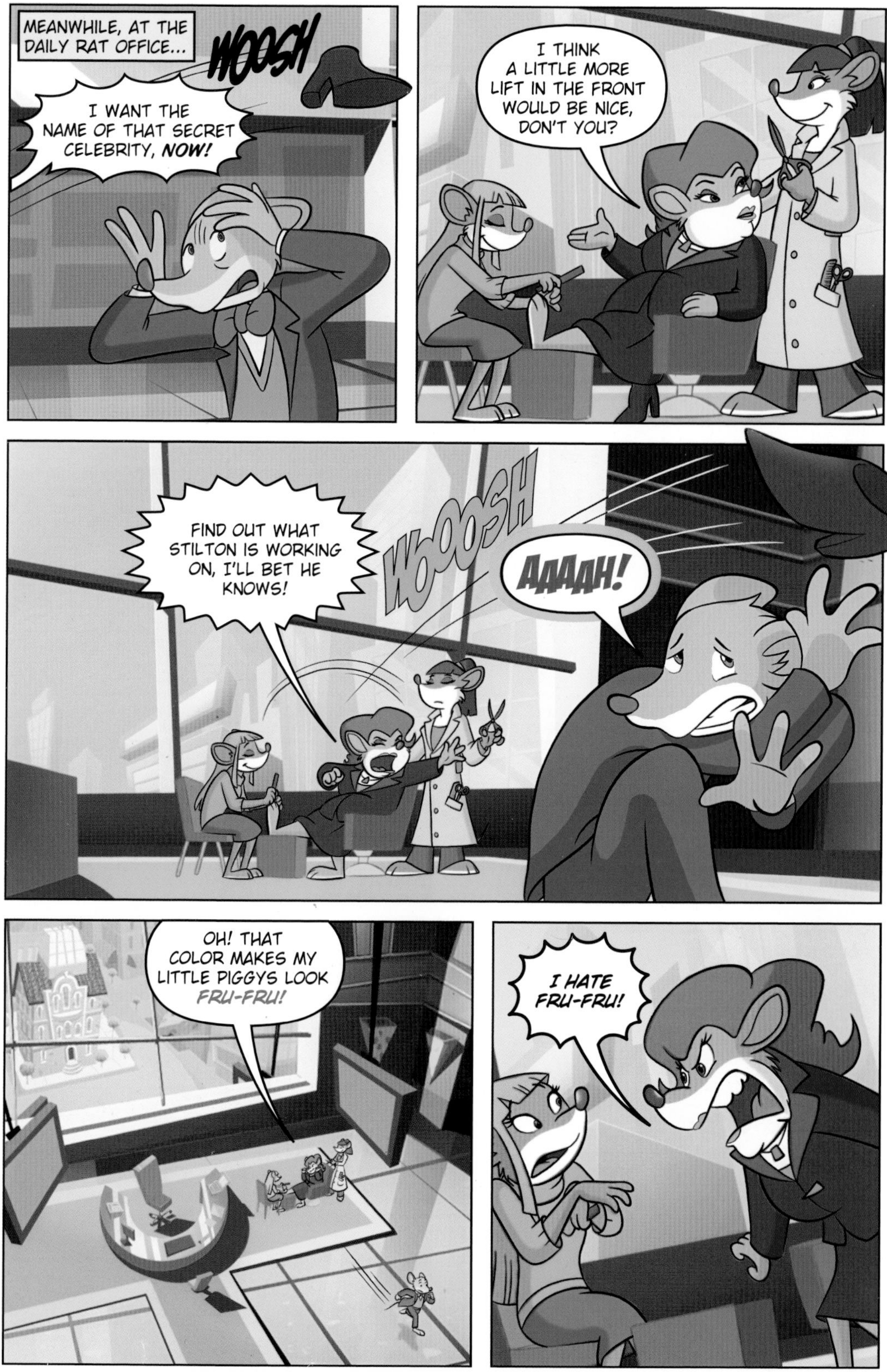
MEANWHILE, AT THE DAILY RAT OFFICE...
WOOSH
I WANT THE NAME OF THAT SECRET CELEBRITY, NOW!
I THINK A LITTLE MORE LIFT IN THE FRONT WOULD BE NICE, DON'T YOU?
FIND OUT WHAT STILTON IS WORKING ON, I'LL BET HE KNOWS!
WOOOSH
AAAAH!
OH! THAT COLOR MAKES MY LITTLE PIGGYS LOOK FRU-FRU!
I HATE FRU-FRU!

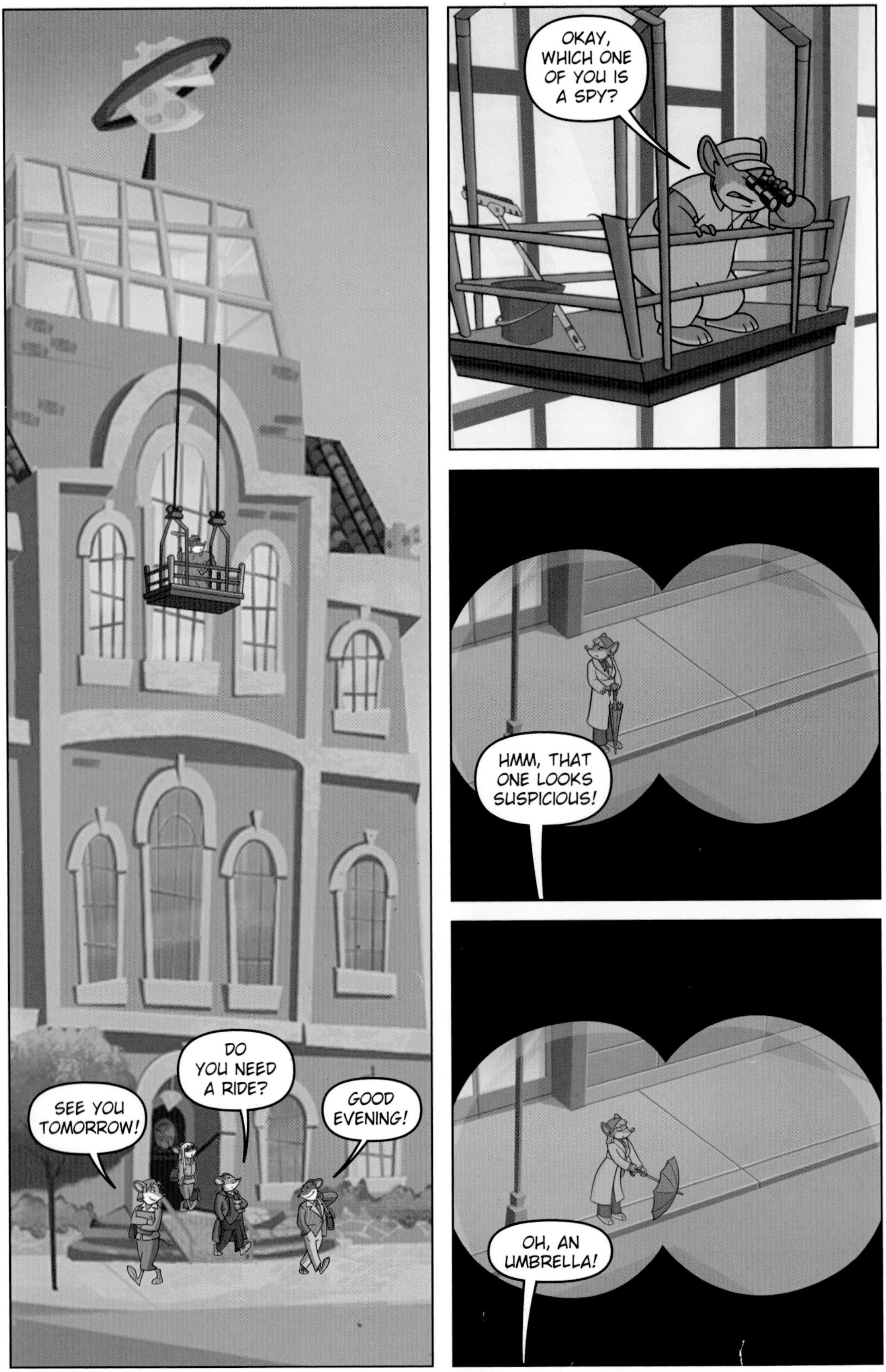
OKAY, WHICH ONE OF YOU IS A SPY?
SEE YOU TOMORROW!
DO YOU NEED A RIDE?
GOOD EVENING!
HMM, THAT ONE LOOKS SUSPICIOUS!
OH, AN UMBRELLA!

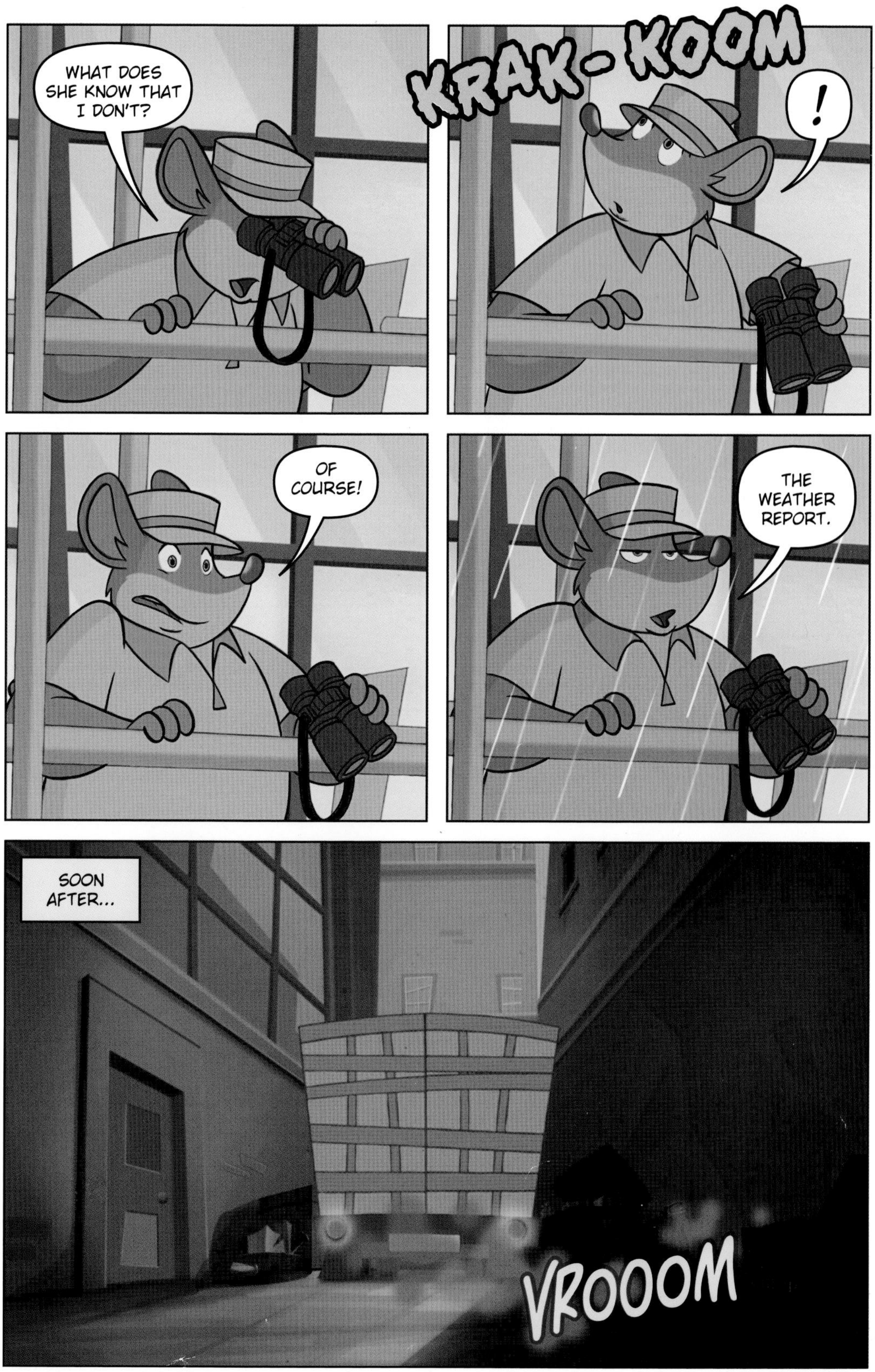
WHAT DOES SHE KNOW THAT I DON'T?
KRAK-KOOM
!
OF COURSE!
THE WEATHER REPORT.
SOON AFTER...
VROOOM

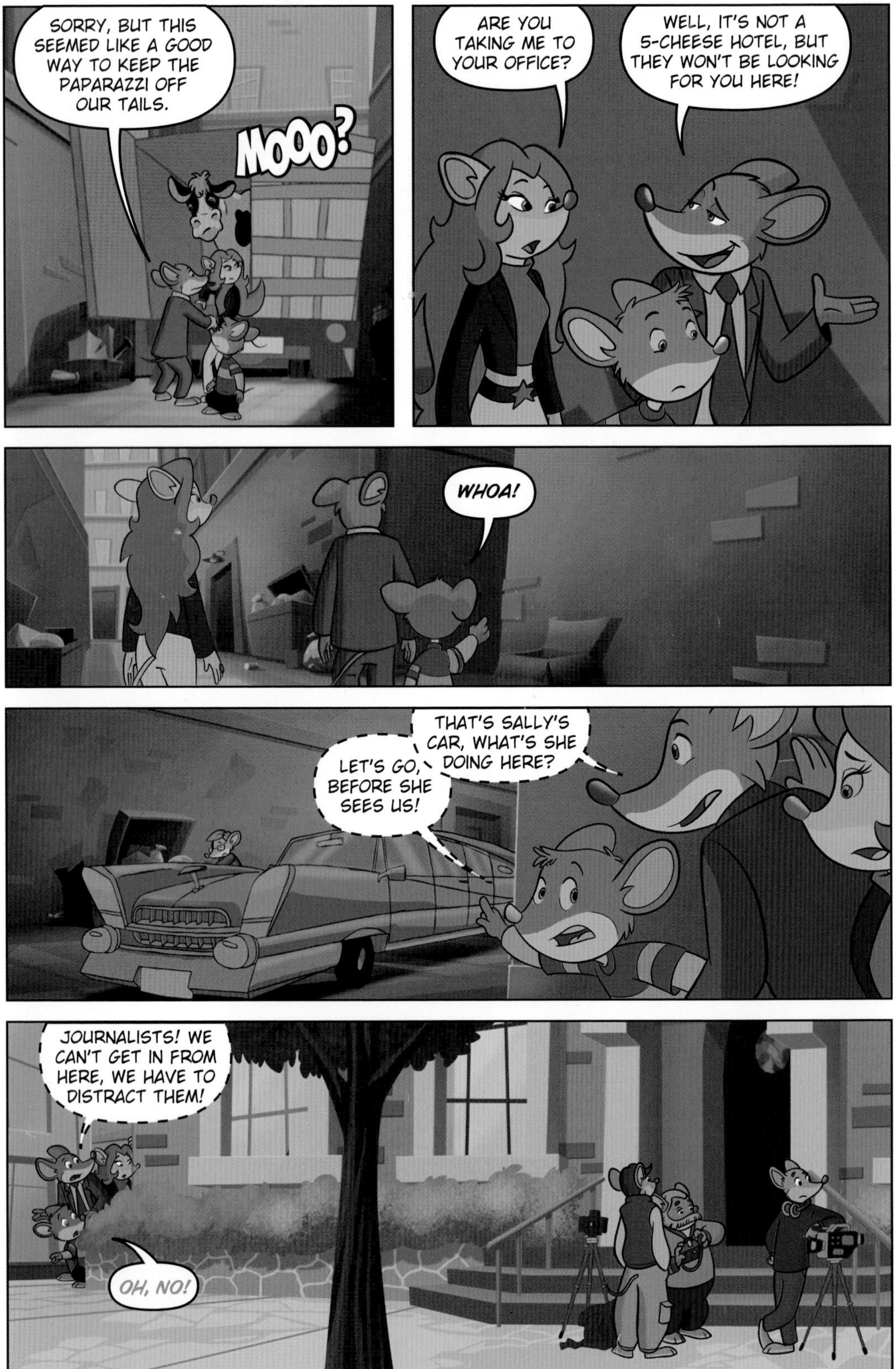
SORRY, BUT THIS SEEMED LIKE A GOOD WAY TO KEEP THE PAPARAZZI OFF OUR TAILS.
MOOO?
ARE YOU TAKING ME TO YOUR OFFICE?
WELL, IT'S NOT A 5-CHEESE HOTEL, BUT THEY WON'T BE LOOKING FOR YOU HERE!
WHOA!
THAT'S SALLY'S CAR, WHAT'S SHE DOING HERE?
LET'S GO, BEFORE SHE SEES US!
JOURNALISTS! WE CAN'T GET IN FROM HERE, WE HAVE TO DISTRACT THEM!
OH, NO!

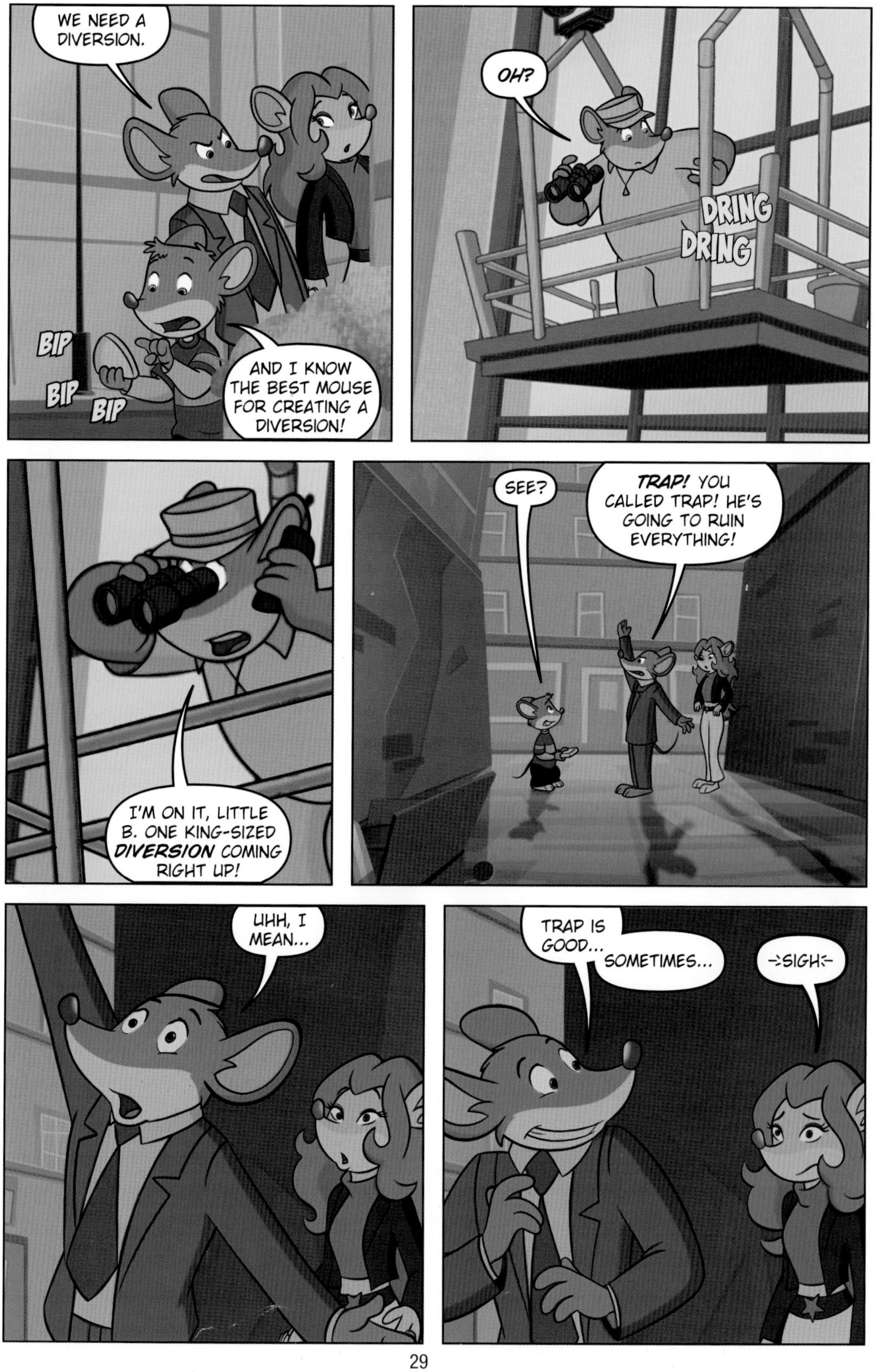
WE NEED A DIVERSION.
BIP
BIP
BIP
AND I KNOW THE BEST MOUSE FOR CREATING A DIVERSION!
OH?
DRING
DRING
I'M ON IT, LITTLE B. ONE KING-SIZED DIVERSION COMING RIGHT UP!
SEE?
TRAP! YOU CALLED TRAP! HE'S GOING TO RUIN EVERYTHING!
UHH, I MEAN...
TRAP IS GOOD...
SOMETIMES...
-SIGH-

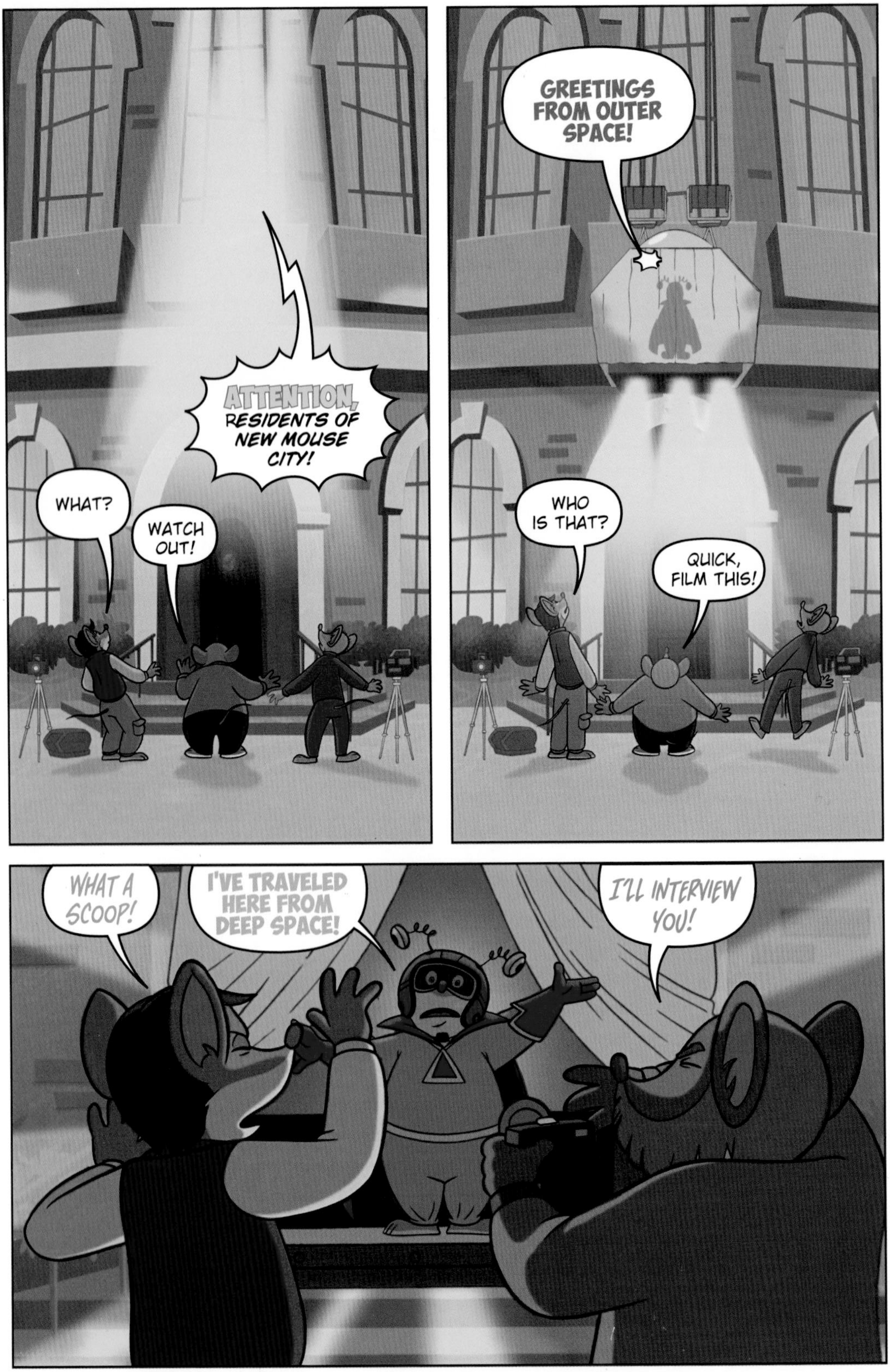
ATTENTION, RESIDENTS OF NEW MOUSE CITY!
WHAT?
WATCH OUT!
GREETINGS FROM OUTER SPACE!
WHO IS THAT?
QUICK, FILM THIS!
WHAT A SCOOP!
I'VE TRAVELED HERE FROM DEEP SPACE!
I'LL INTERVIEW YOU!

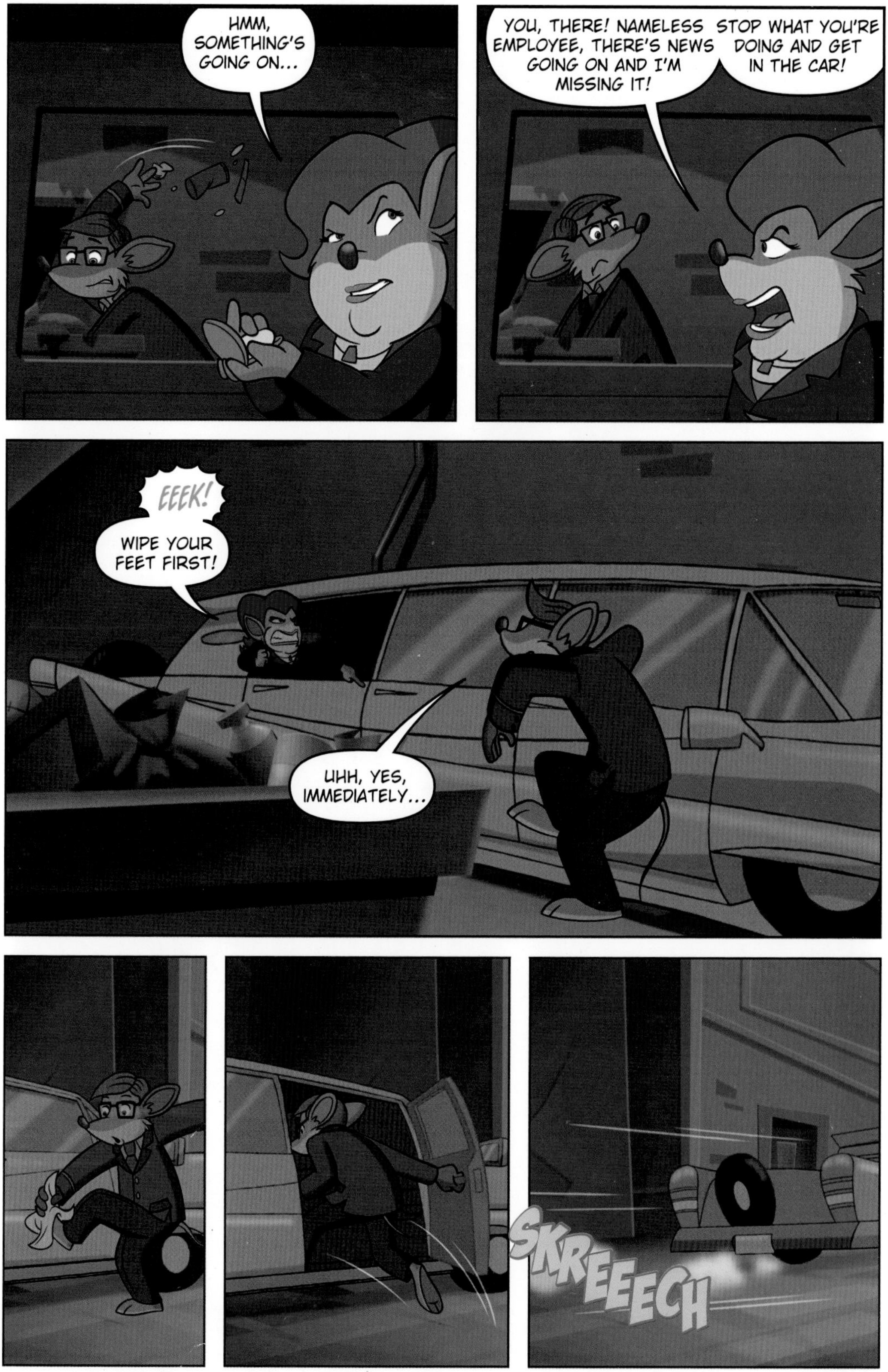
HMM, SOMETHING'S GOING ON...
YOU, THERE! NAMELESS EMPLOYEE, THERE'S NEWS GOING ON AND I'M MISSING IT!
STOP WHAT YOU'RE DOING AND GET IN THE CAR!
EEEK!
WIPE YOUR FEET FIRST!
UHH, YES, IMMEDIATELY...
SKREEECH

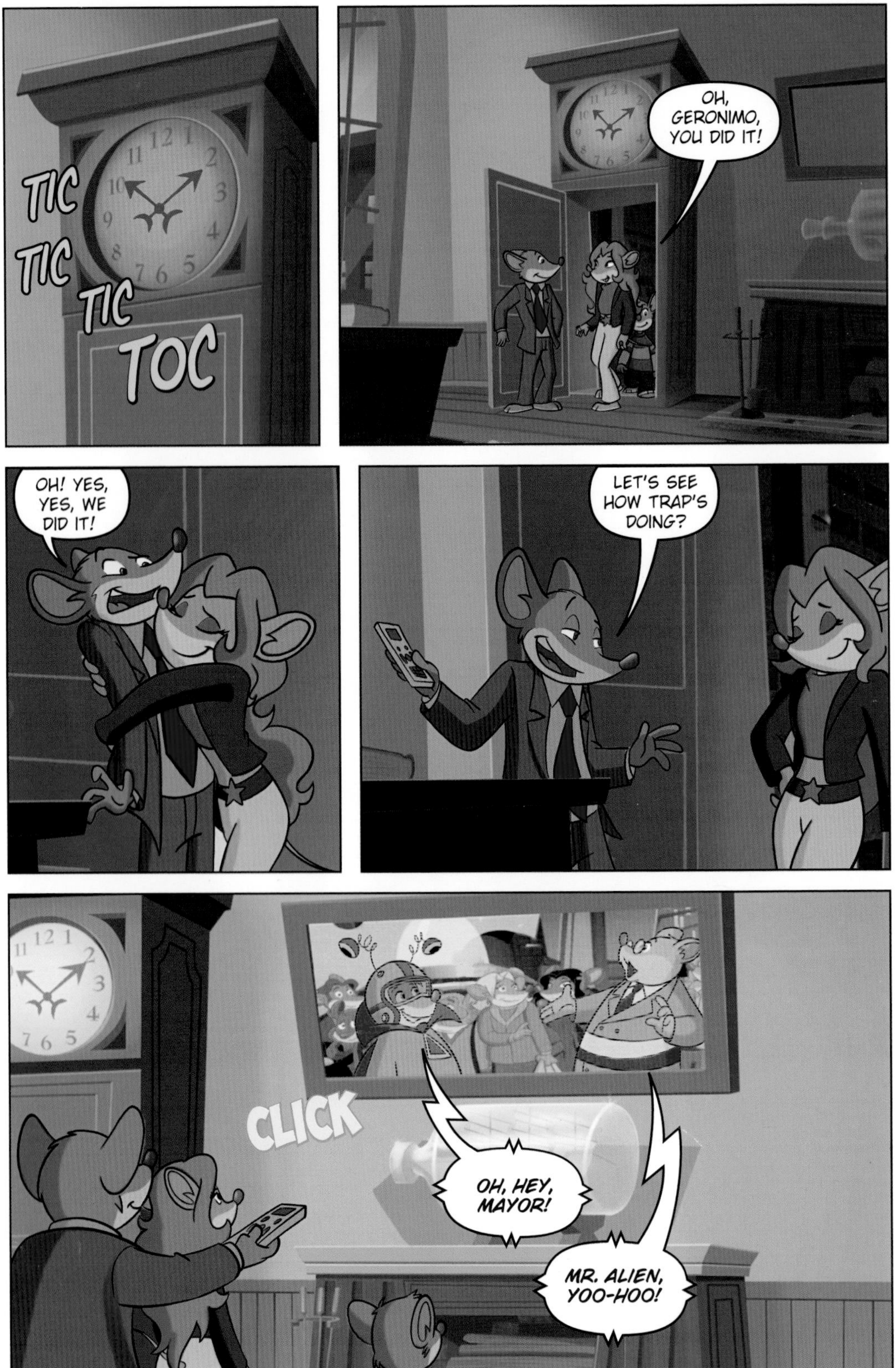
TIC
TIC
TIC
TOC
OH, GERONIMO, YOU DID IT!
OH! YES, YES, WE DID IT!
LET'S SEE HOW TRAP'S DOING?
CLICK
OH, HEY, MAYOR!
MR. ALIEN, YOO-HOO!

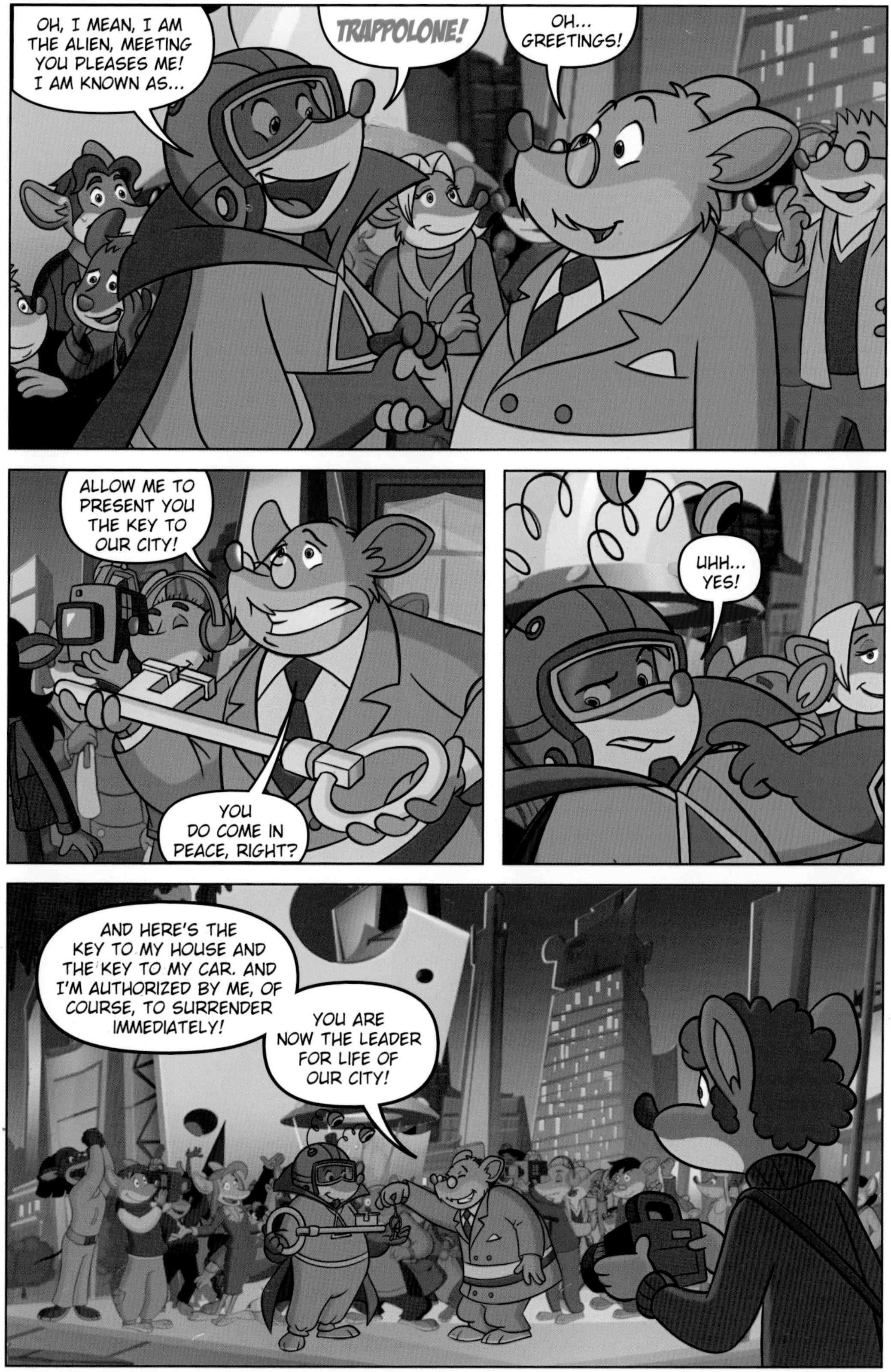

OH, I MEAN, I AM THE ALIEN, MEETING YOU PLEASES ME! I AM KNOWN AS...
TRAPPOLONE!
OH... GREETINGS!
ALLOW ME TO PRESENT YOU THE KEY TO OUR CITY!
YOU DO COME IN PEACE, RIGHT?
UHH... YES!
AND HERE'S THE KEY TO MY HOUSE AND THE KEY TO MY CAR. AND I'M AUTHORIZED BY ME, OF COURSE, TO SURRENDER IMMEDIATELY!
YOU ARE NOW THE LEADER FOR LIFE OF OUR CITY!

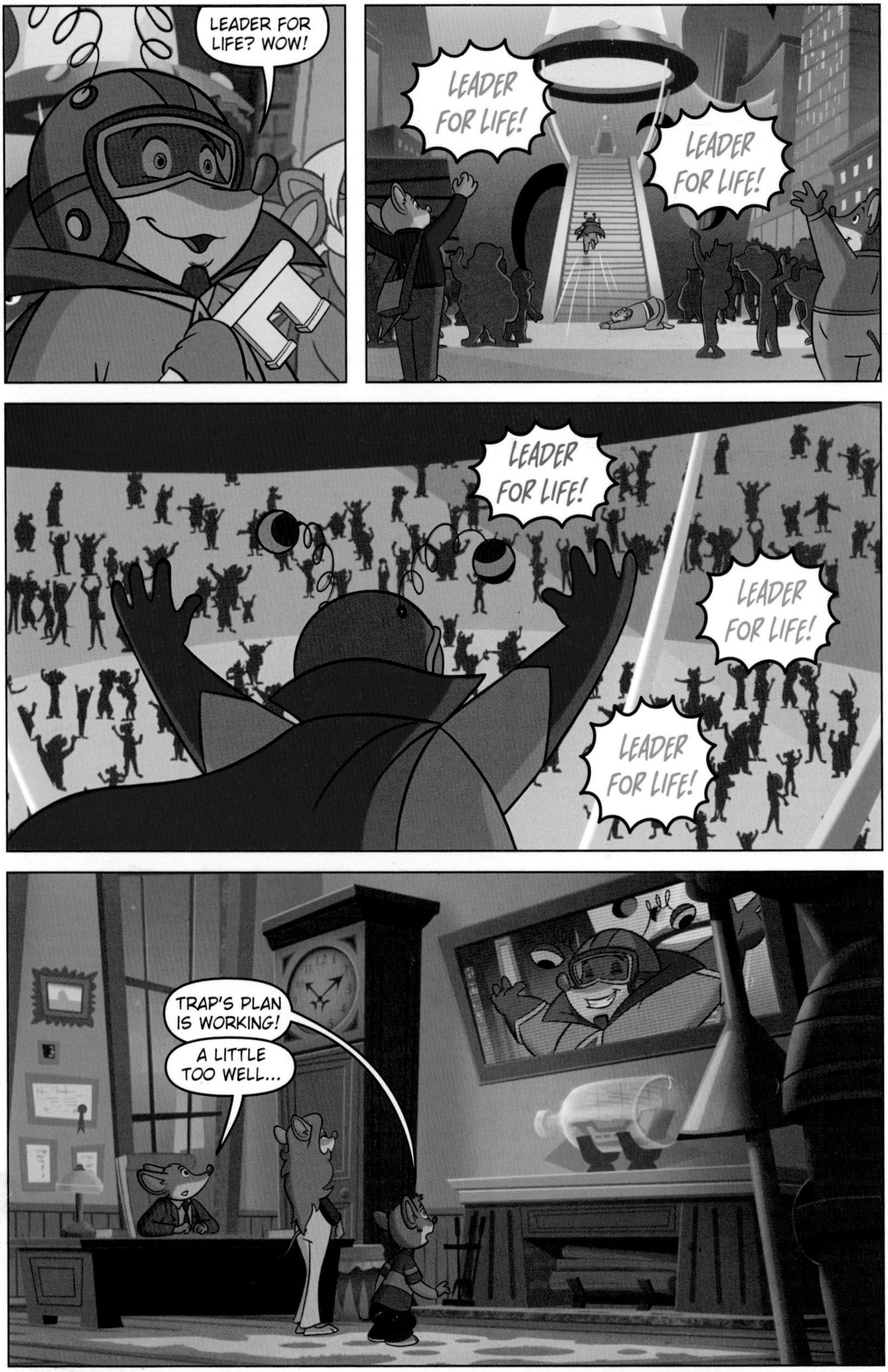
LEADER FOR LIFE? WOW!
LEADER FOR LIFE!
LEADER FOR LIFE!
LEADER FOR LIFE!
LEADER FOR LIFE!
LEADER FOR LIFE!
TRAP'S PLAN IS WORKING!
A LITTLE TOO WELL...

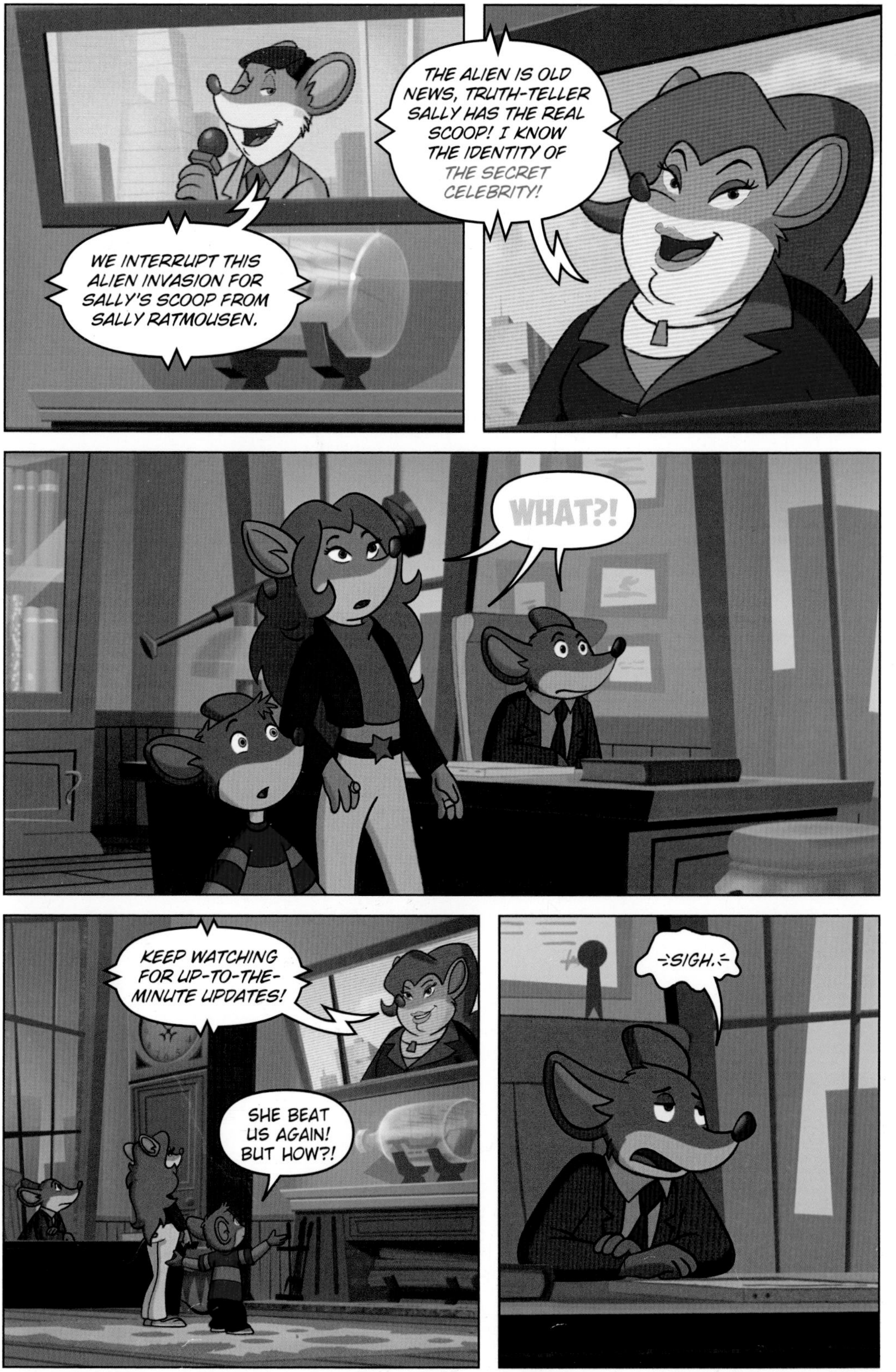
WE INTERRUPT THIS ALIEN INVASION FOR SALLY'S SCOOP FROM SALLY RATMOUSEN.
THE ALIEN IS OLD NEWS, TRUTH-TELLER SALLY HAS THE REAL SCOOP! I KNOW THE IDENTITY OF THE SECRET CELEBRITY!
WHAT?!
KEEP WATCHING FOR UP-TO-THE-MINUTE UPDATES!
SHE BEAT US AGAIN! BUT HOW?!
SIGH.

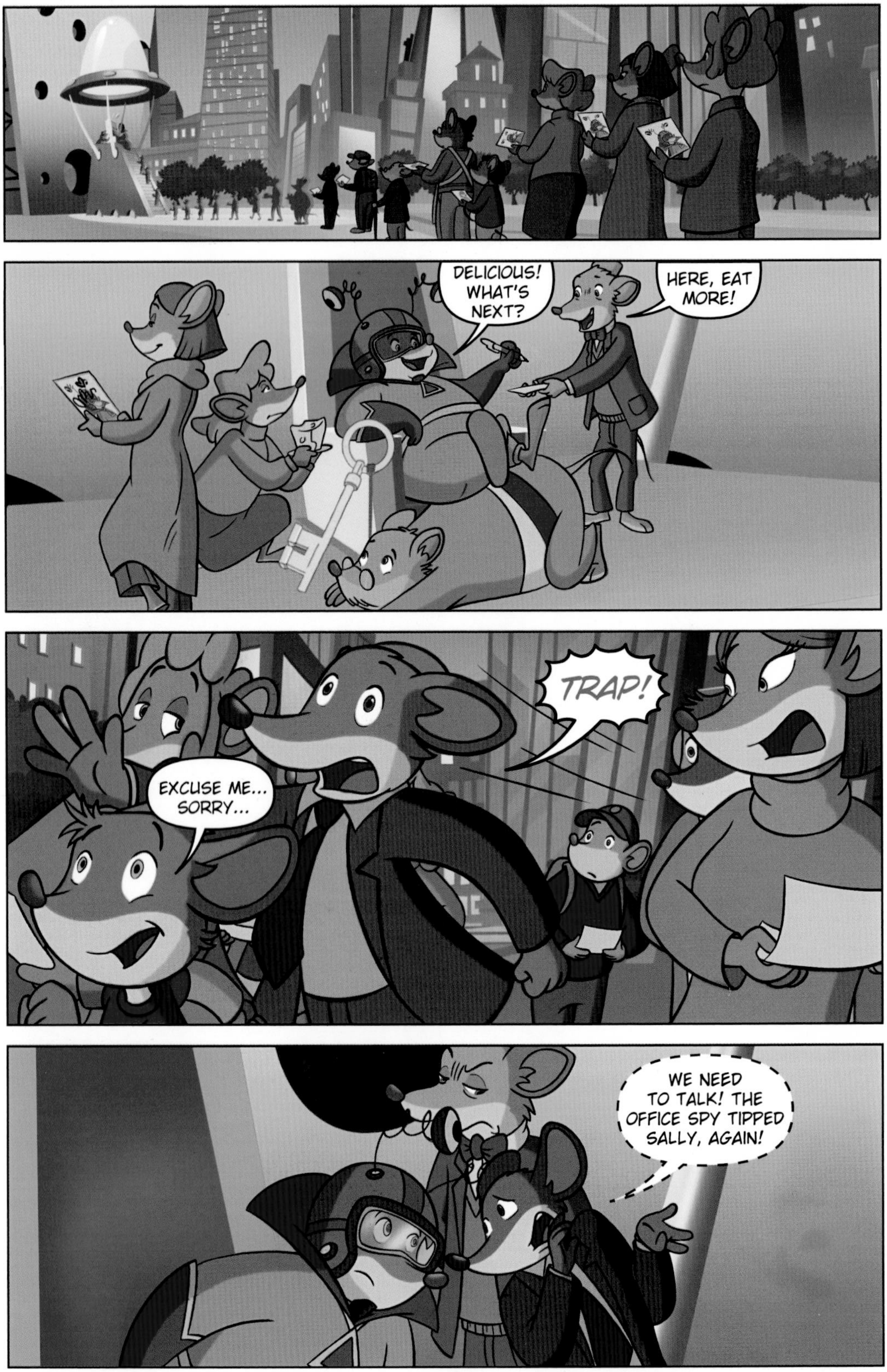
DELICIOUS! WHAT'S NEXT?
HERE, EAT MORE!
EXCUSE ME... SORRY...
TRAP!
WE NEED TO TALK! THE OFFICE SPY TIPPED SALLY, AGAIN!

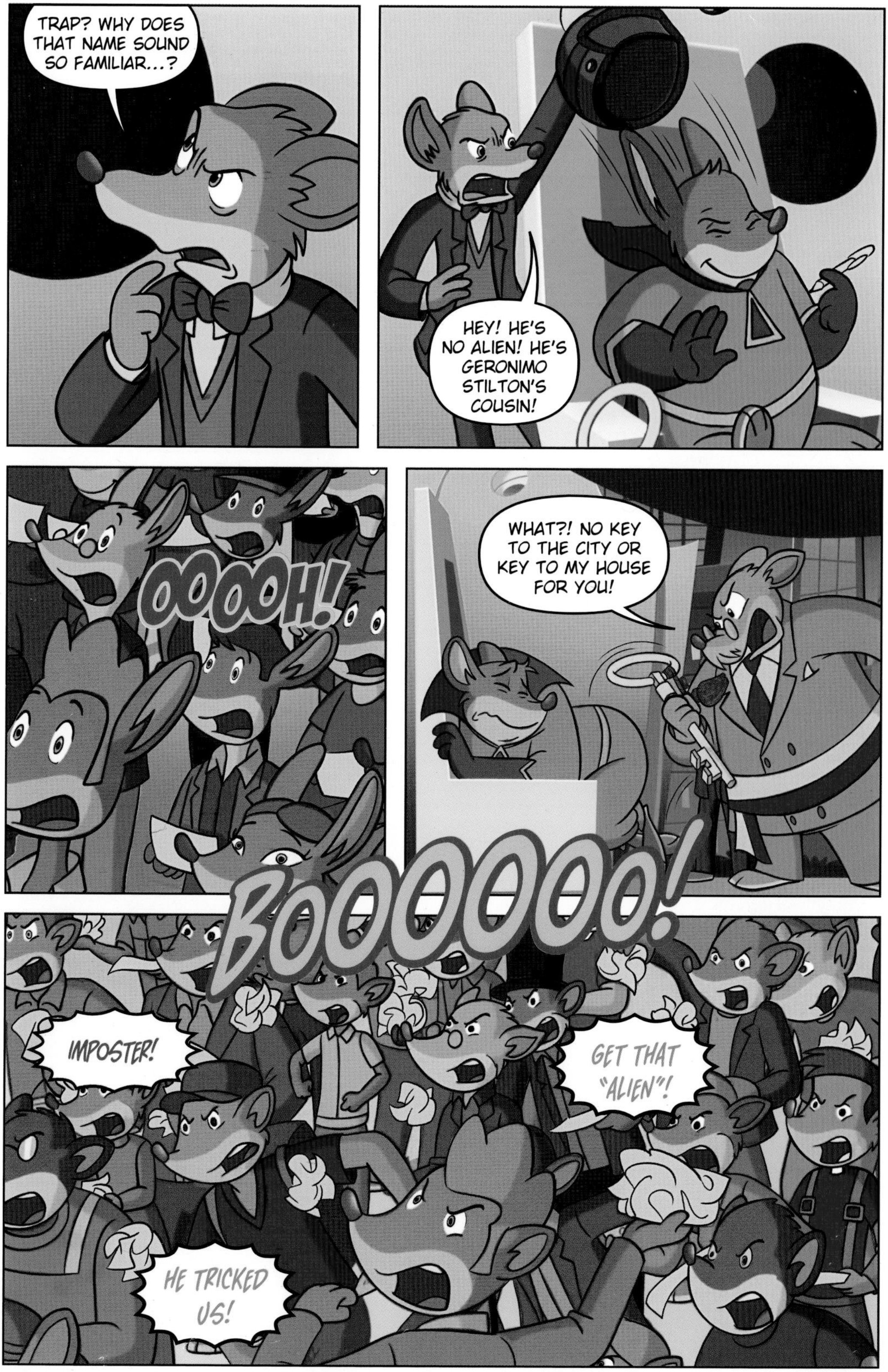
TRAP? WHY DOES THAT NAME SOUND SO FAMILIAR...?
HEY! HE'S NO ALIEN! HE'S GERONIMO STILTON'S COUSIN!
OOOOH!
WHAT?! NO KEY TO THE CITY OR KEY TO MY HOUSE FOR YOU!
BOOOOOO!
IMPOSTER!
GET THAT "ALIEN"!
HE TRICKED US!

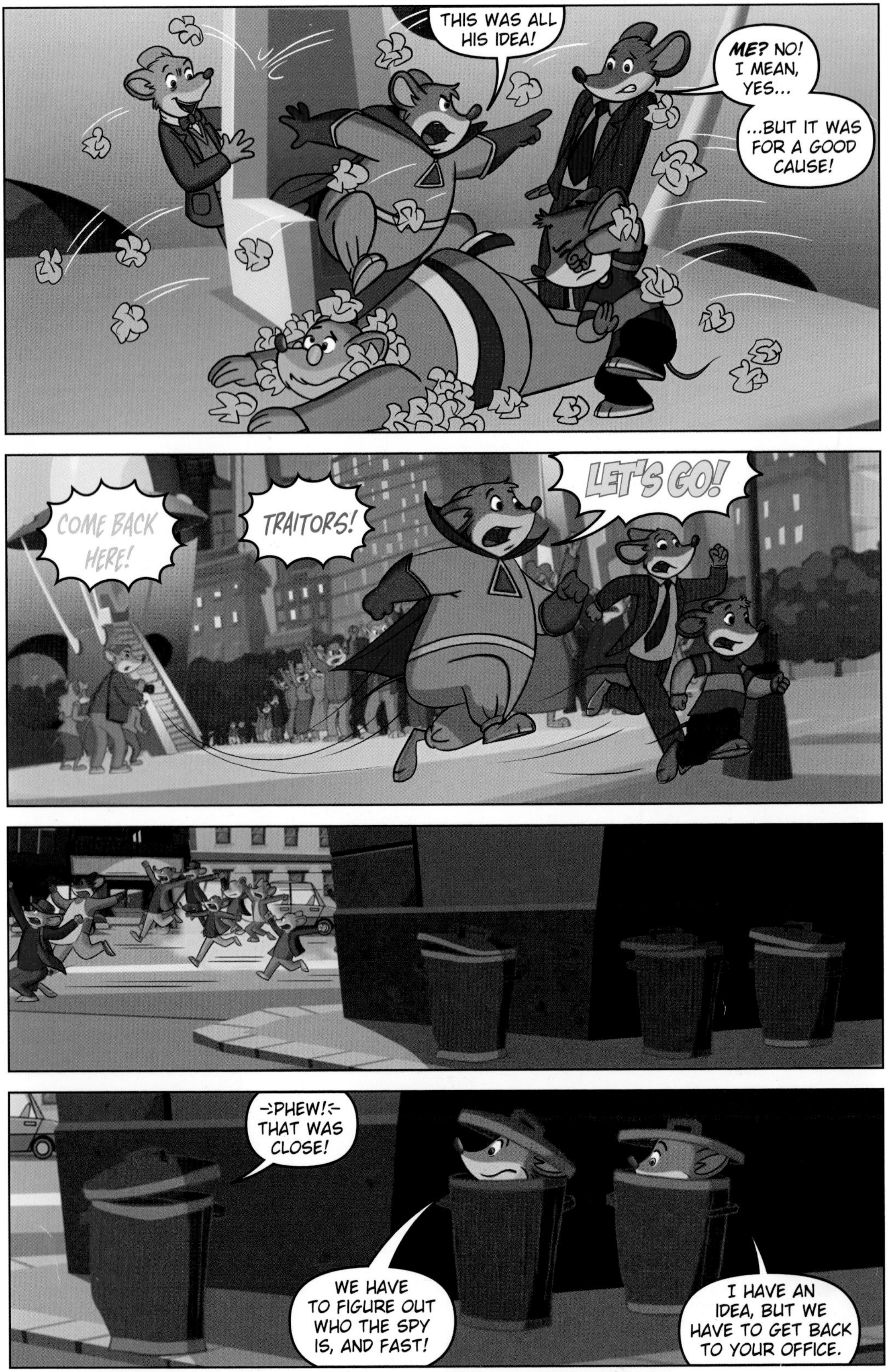
THIS WAS ALL HIS IDEA!
ME? NO! I MEAN, YES...
...BUT IT WAS FOR A GOOD CAUSE!
COME BACK HERE!
TRAITORS!
LET'S GO!
PHEW! THAT WAS CLOSE!
WE HAVE TO FIGURE OUT WHO THE SPY IS, AND FAST!
I HAVE AN IDEA, BUT WE HAVE TO GET BACK TO YOUR OFFICE.

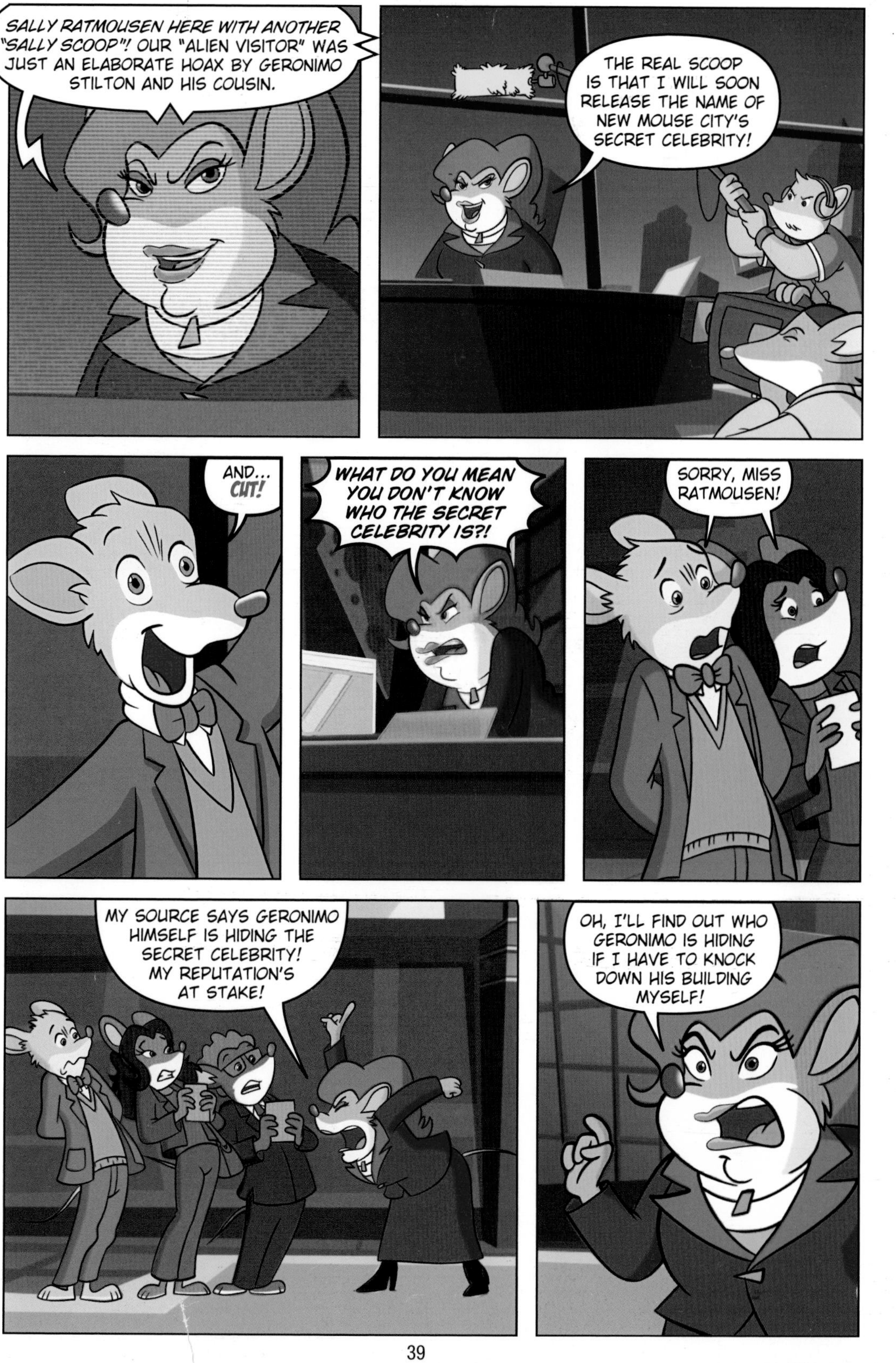
SALLY RATMOUSEN HERE WITH ANOTHER "SALLY SCOOP"! OUR "ALIEN VISITOR" WAS JUST AN ELABORATE HOAX BY GERONIMO STILTON AND HIS COUSIN.
THE REAL SCOOP IS THAT I WILL SOON RELEASE THE NAME OF NEW MOUSE CITY'S SECRET CELEBRITY!
AND... CUT!
WHAT DO YOU MEAN YOU DON'T KNOW WHO THE SECRET CELEBRITY IS?!
SORRY, MISS RATMOUSEN!
MY SOURCE SAYS GERONIMO HIMSELF IS HIDING THE SECRET CELEBRITY! MY REPUTATION'S AT STAKE!
OH, I'LL FIND OUT WHO GERONIMO IS HIDING IF I HAVE TO KNOCK DOWN HIS BUILDING MYSELF!

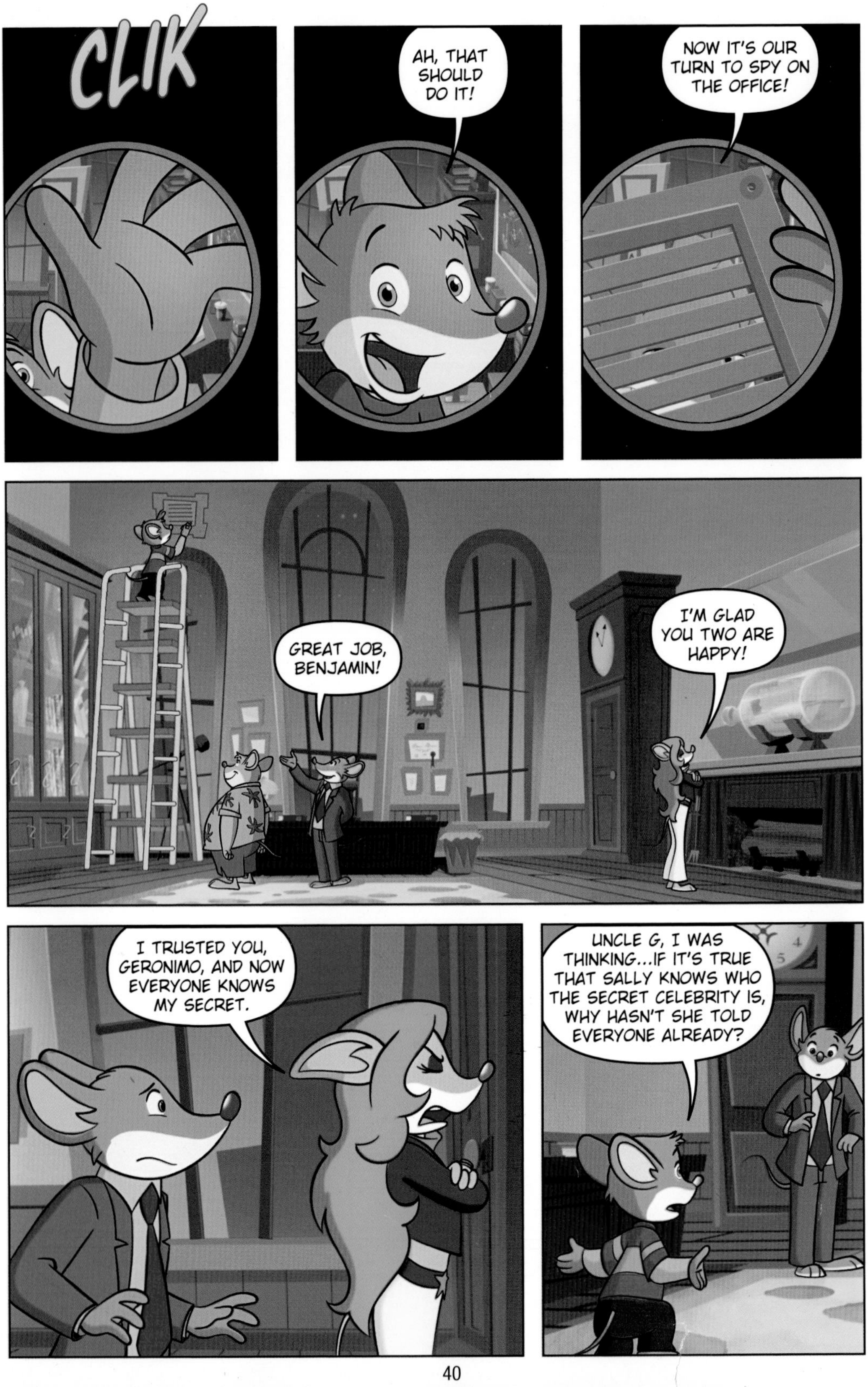
CLIK
AH, THAT SHOULD DO IT!
NOW IT'S OUR TURN TO SPY ON THE OFFICE!
GREAT JOB, BENJAMIN!
I'M GLAD YOU TWO ARE HAPPY!
I TRUSTED YOU, GERONIMO, AND NOW EVERYONE KNOWS MY SECRET.
UNCLE G, I WAS THINKING...IF IT'S TRUE THAT SALLY KNOWS WHO THE SECRET CELEBRITY IS, WHY HASN'T SHE TOLD EVERYONE ALREADY?

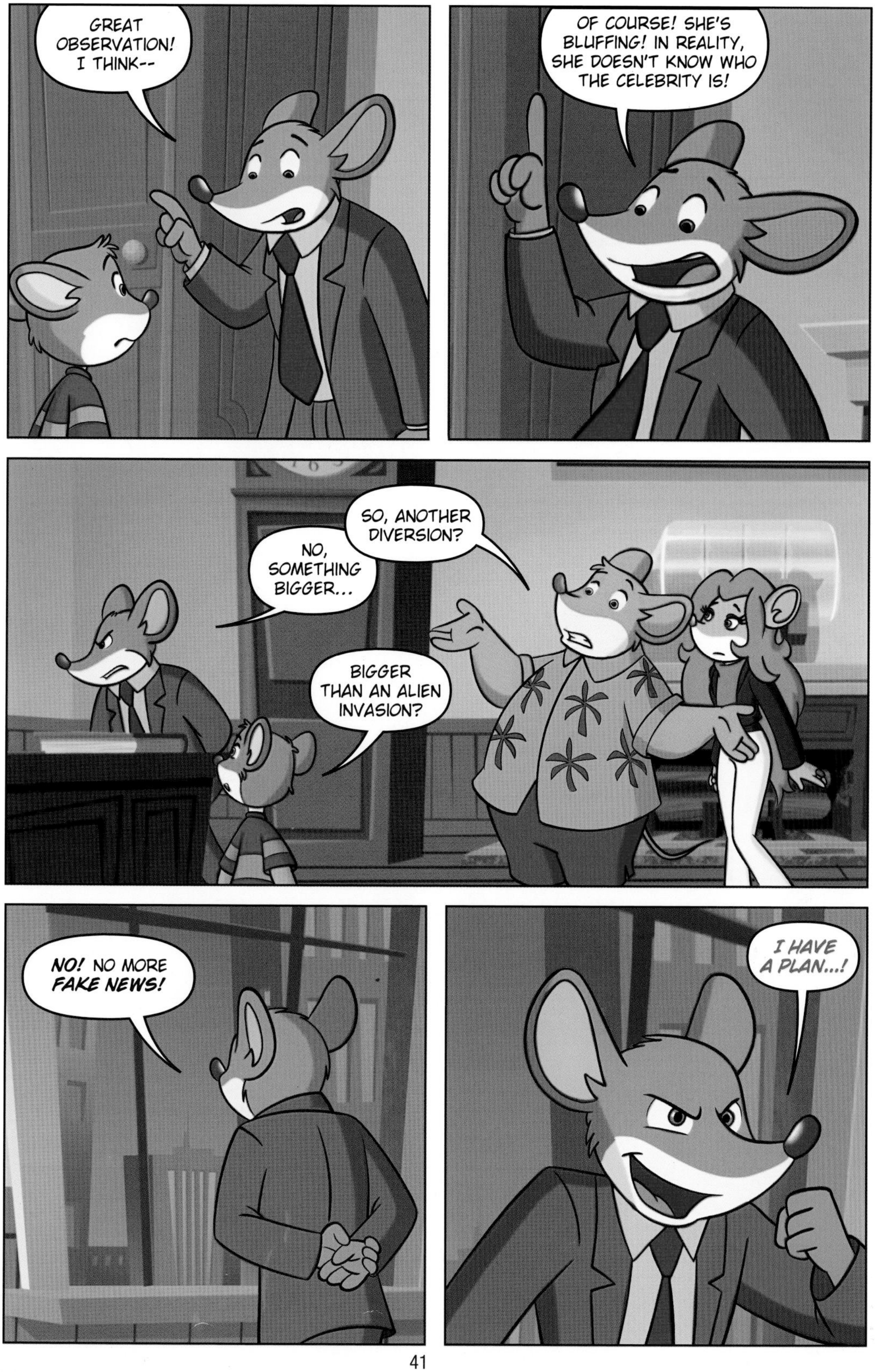
GREAT OBSERVATION! I THINK--
OF COURSE! SHE'S BLUFFING! IN REALITY, SHE DOESN'T KNOW WHO THE CELEBRITY IS!
SO, ANOTHER DIVERSION?
NO, SOMETHING BIGGER...
BIGGER THAN AN ALIEN INVASION?
NO! NO MORE FAKE NEWS!
I HAVE A PLAN...!

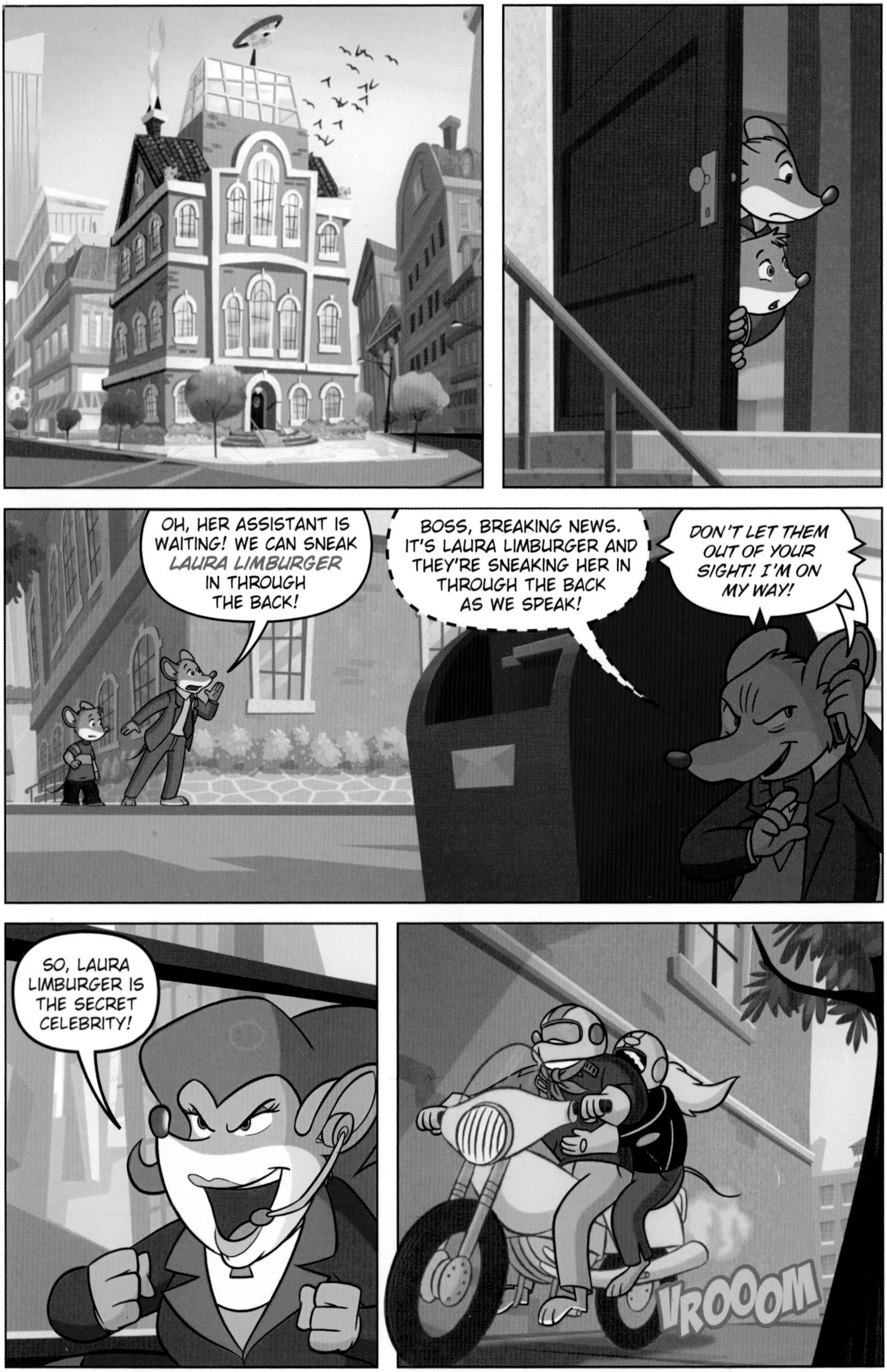
OH, HER ASSISTANT IS WAITING! WE CAN SNEAK LAURA LIMBURGER IN THROUGH THE BACK!
BOSS, BREAKING NEWS. IT'S LAURA LIMBURGER AND THEY'RE SNEAKING HER IN THROUGH THE BACK AS WE SPEAK!
DON'T LET THEM OUT OF YOUR SIGHT! I'M ON MY WAY!
SO, LAURA LIMBURGER IS THE SECRET CELEBRITY!
VROOOM

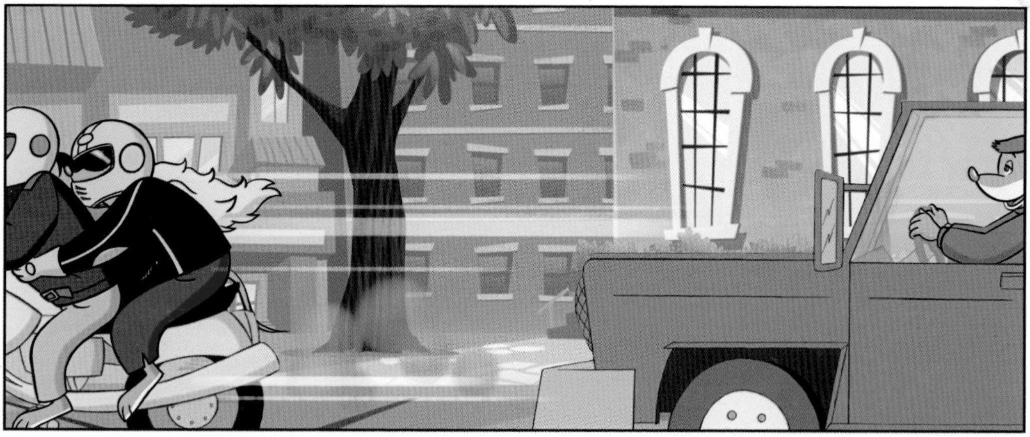

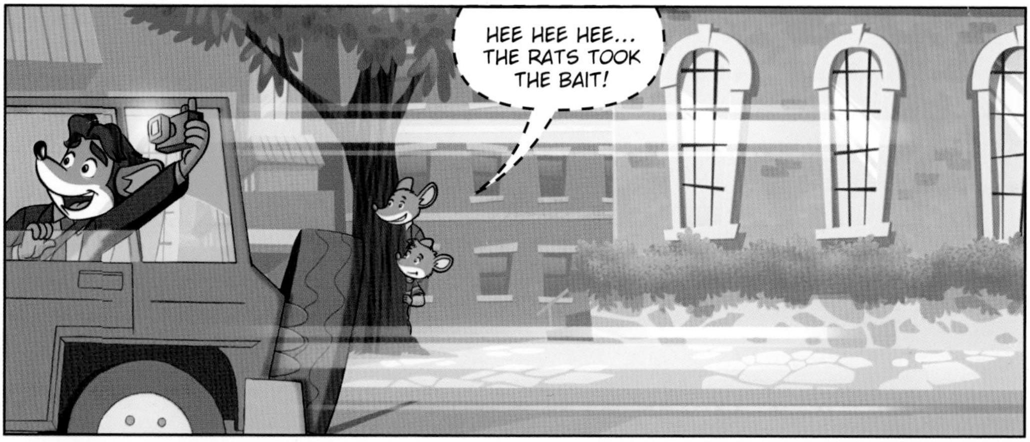
HEE HEE HEE... THE RATS TOOK THE BAIT!

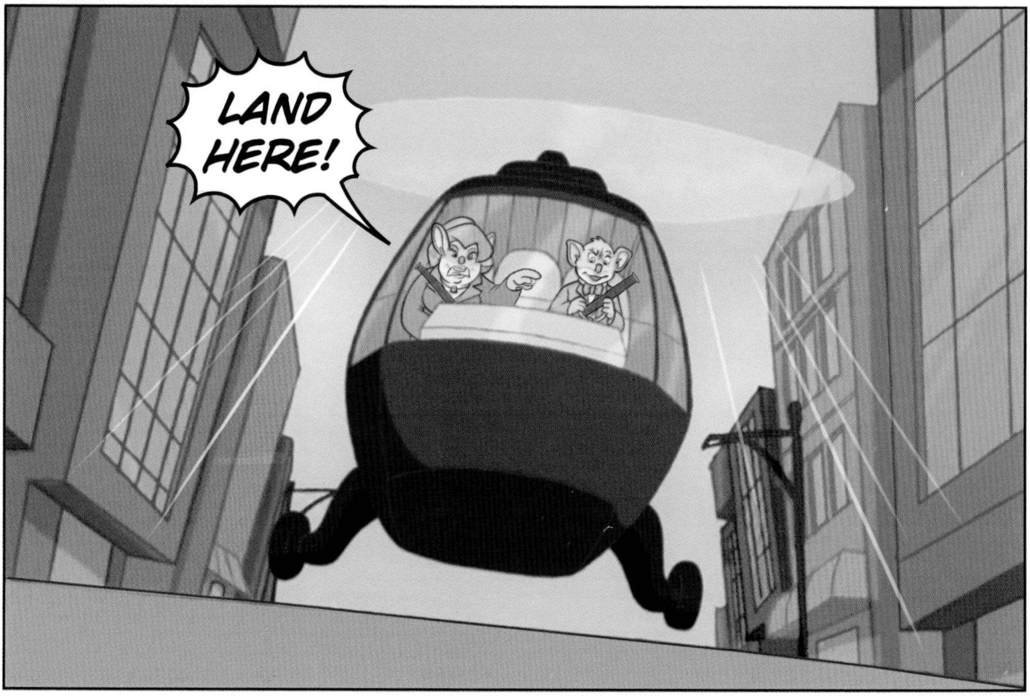
LAND HERE!

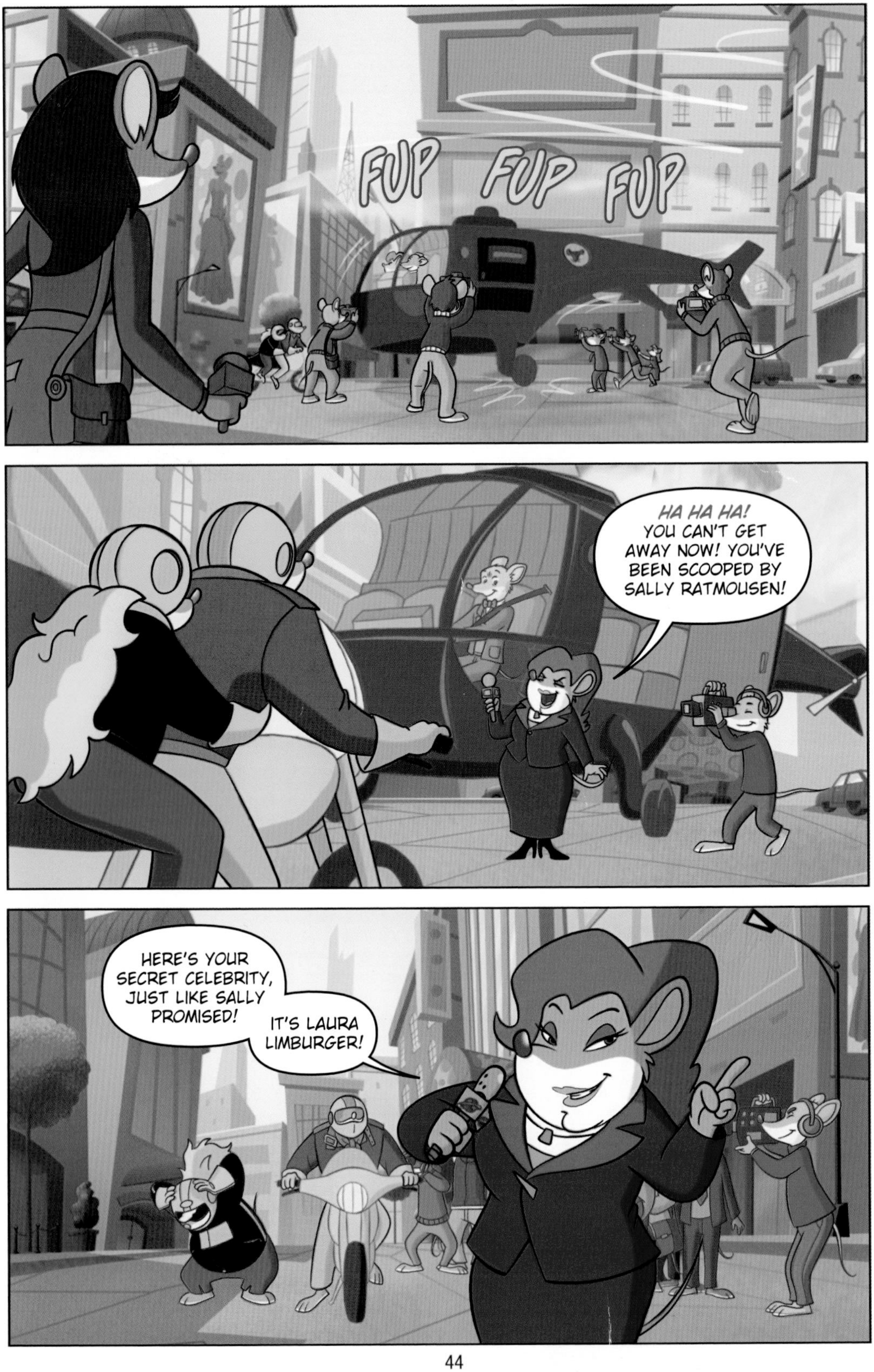
FUP FUP FUP
HA HA HA! YOU CAN'T GET AWAY NOW! YOU'VE BEEN SCOOPED BY SALLY RATMOUSEN!
HERE'S YOUR SECRET CELEBRITY, JUST LIKE SALLY PROMISED!
IT'S LAURA LIMBURGER!

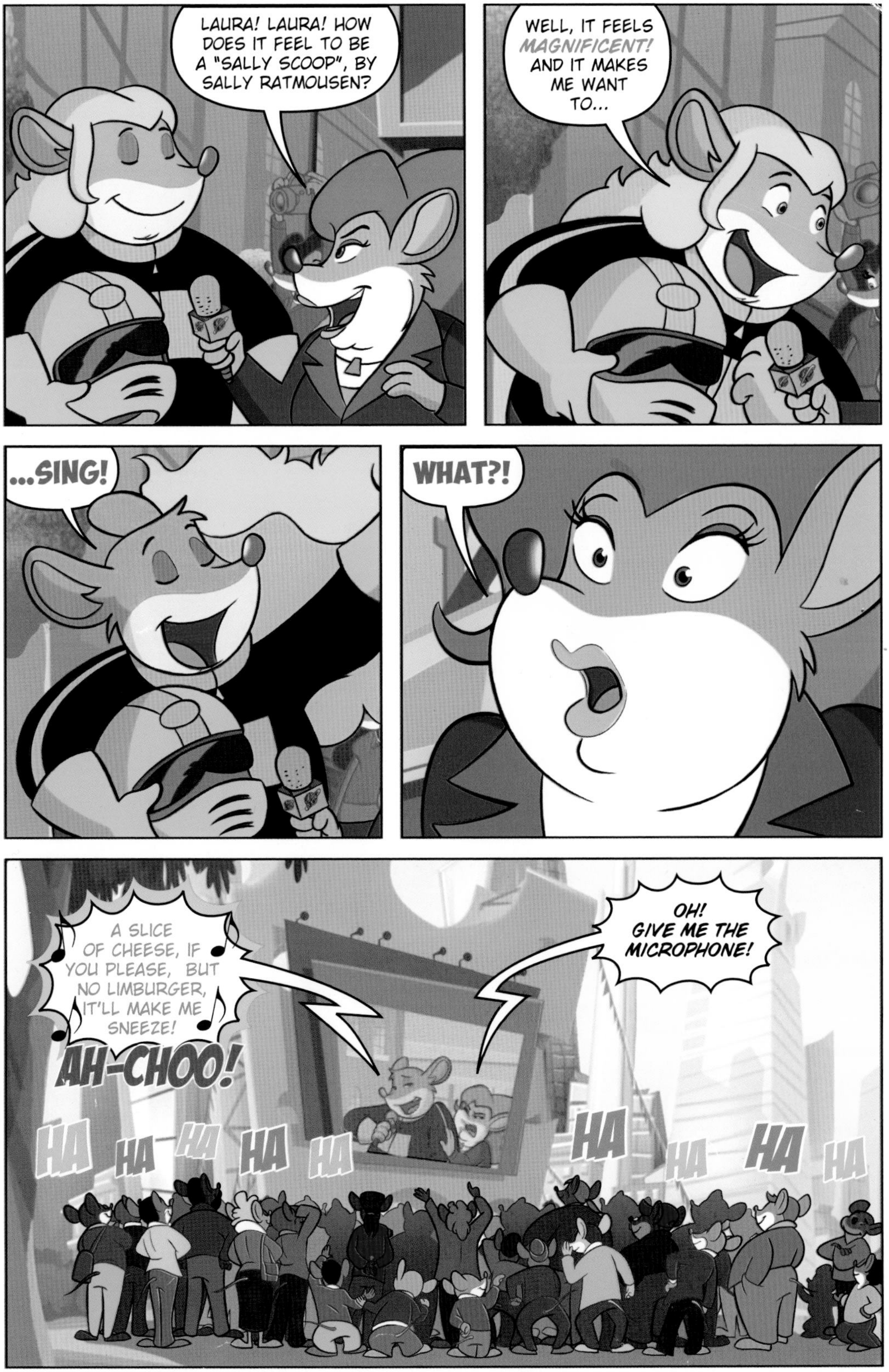
LAURA! LAURA! HOW DOES IT FEEL TO BE A "SALLY SCOOP", BY SALLY RATMOUSEN?
WELL, IT FEELS MAGNIFICENT! AND IT MAKES ME WANT TO...
...SING!
WHAT?!
A SLICE OF CHEESE, IF YOU PLEASE, BUT NO LIMBURGER, IT'LL MAKE ME SNEEZE!
AH-CHOO!
OH! GIVE ME THE MICROPHONE!
HA HA HA HA HA HA HA HA HA

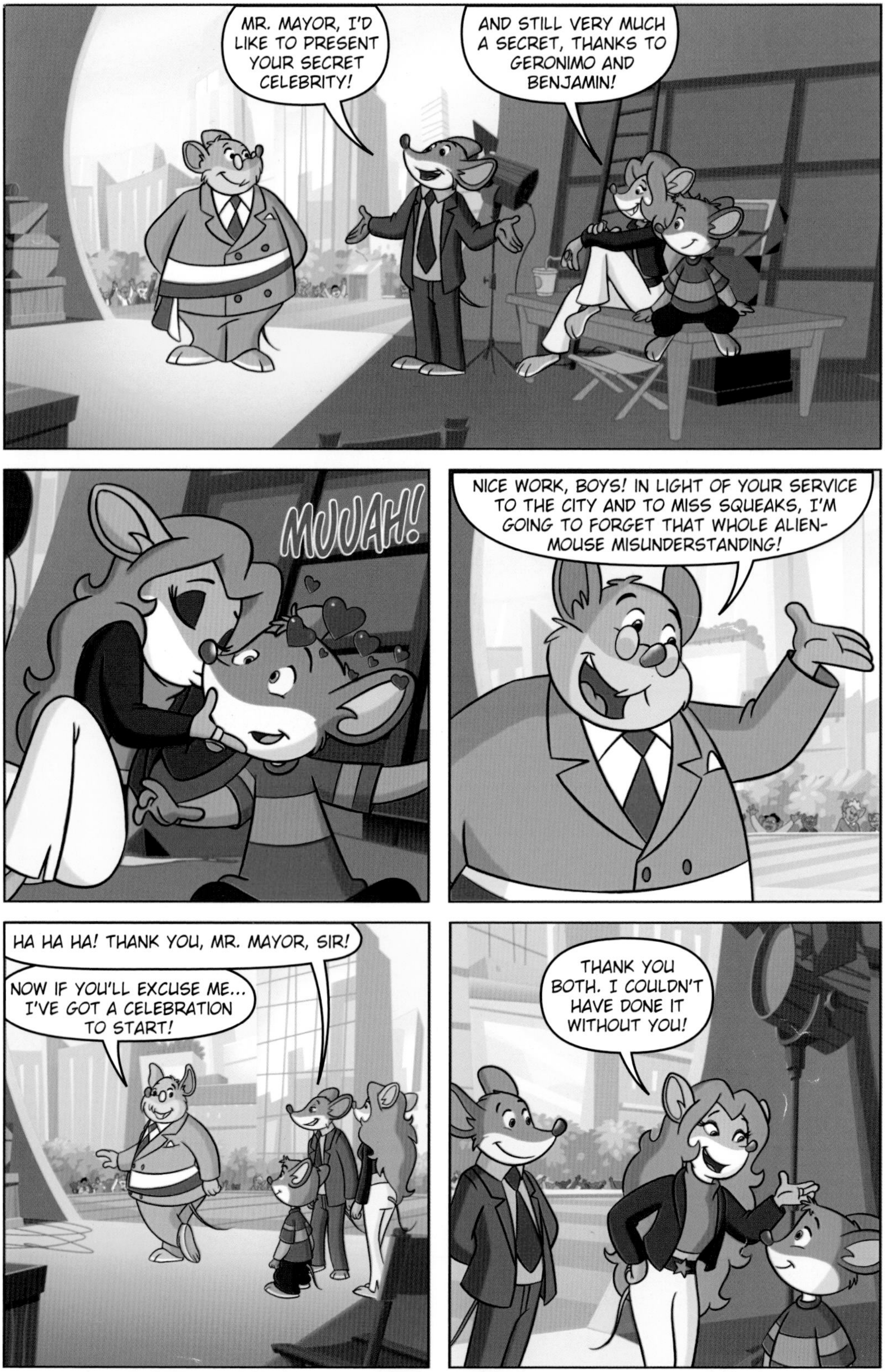
MR. MAYOR, I'D LIKE TO PRESENT YOUR SECRET CELEBRITY!
AND STILL VERY MUCH A SECRET, THANKS TO GERONIMO AND BENJAMIN!
MUUAH!
NICE WORK, BOYS! IN LIGHT OF YOUR SERVICE TO THE CITY AND TO MISS SQUEAKS, I'M GOING TO FORGET THAT WHOLE ALIEN-MOUSE MISUNDERSTANDING!
HA HA HA! THANK YOU, MR. MAYOR, SIR!
NOW IF YOU'LL EXCUSE ME... I'VE GOT A CELEBRATION TO START!
THANK YOU BOTH. I COULDN'T HAVE DONE IT WITHOUT YOU!

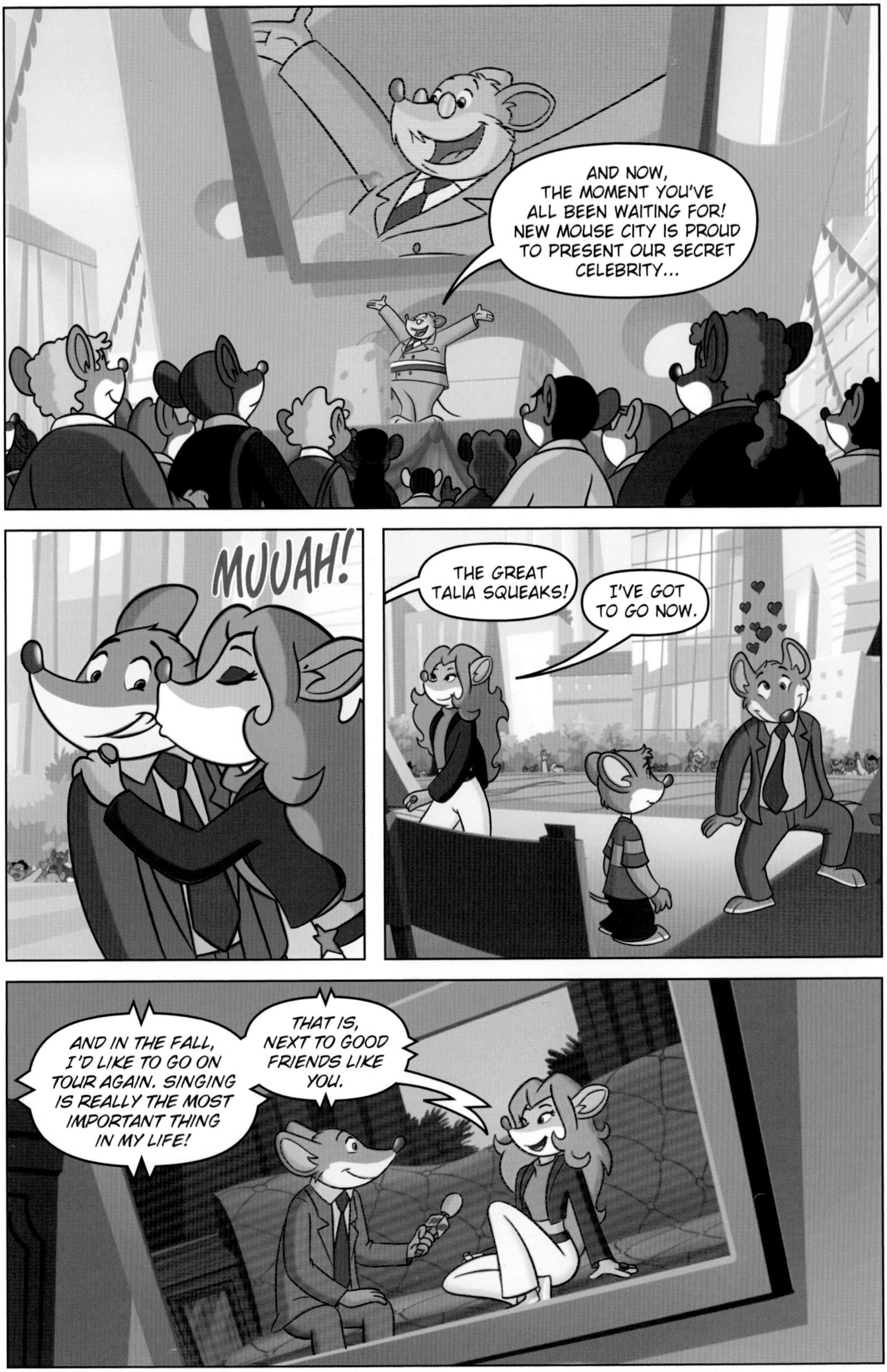
AND NOW, THE MOMENT YOU'VE ALL BEEN WAITING FOR! NEW MOUSE CITY IS PROUD TO PRESENT OUR SECRET CELEBRITY...
MUUAH!
THE GREAT TALIA SQUEAKS!
I'VE GOT TO GO NOW.
AND IN THE FALL, I'D LIKE TO GO ON TOUR AGAIN. SINGING IS REALLY THE MOST IMPORTANT THING IN MY LIFE!
THAT IS, NEXT TO GOOD FRIENDS LIKE YOU.

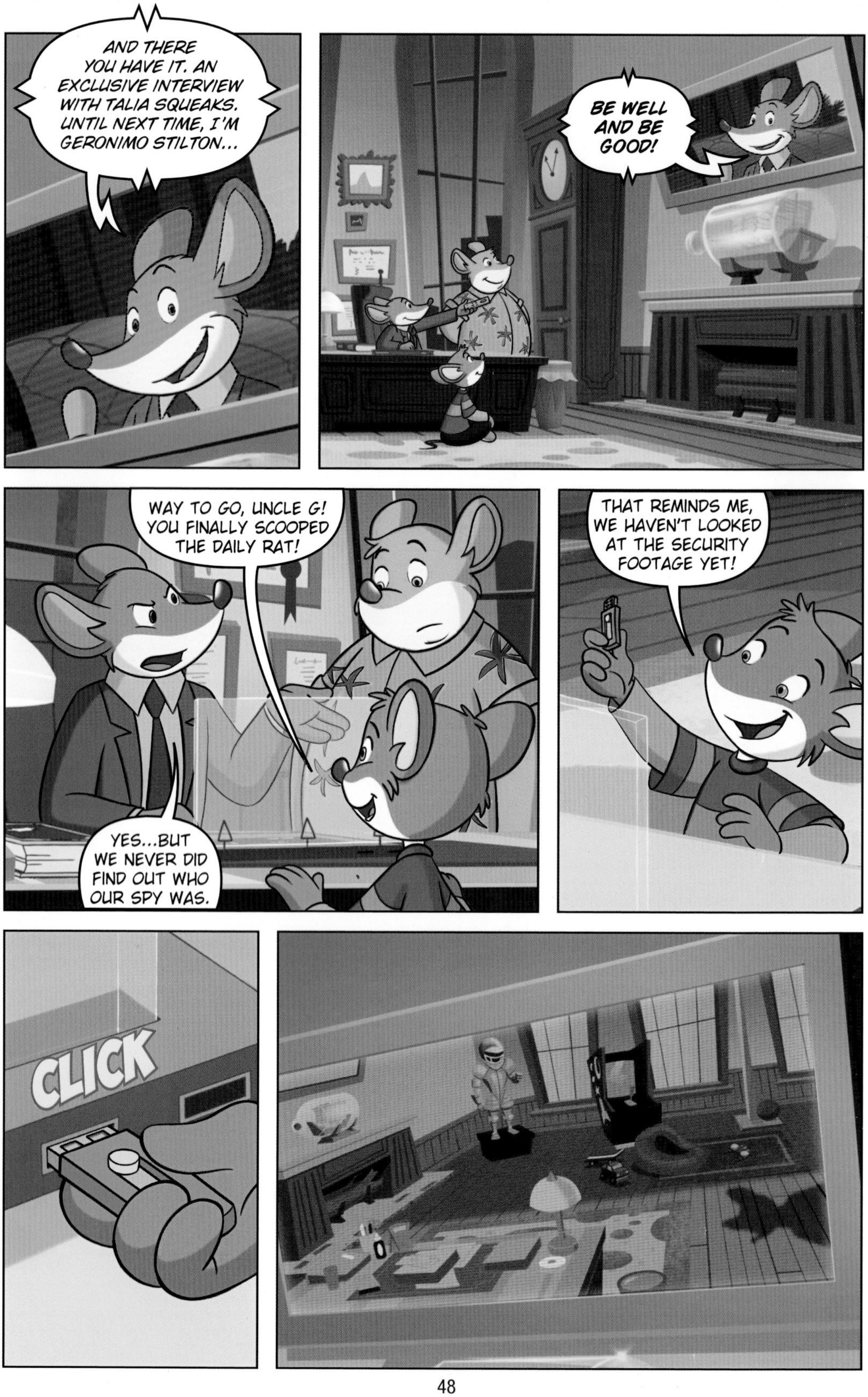
AND THERE YOU HAVE IT. AN EXCLUSIVE INTERVIEW WITH TALIA SQUEAKS. UNTIL NEXT TIME, I'M GERONIMO STILTON...
BE WELL AND BE GOOD!
WAY TO GO, UNCLE G! YOU FINALLY SCOOPED THE DAILY RAT!
YES...BUT WE NEVER DID FIND OUT WHO OUR SPY WAS.
THAT REMINDS ME, WE HAVEN'T LOOKED AT THE SECURITY FOOTAGE YET!
CLICK

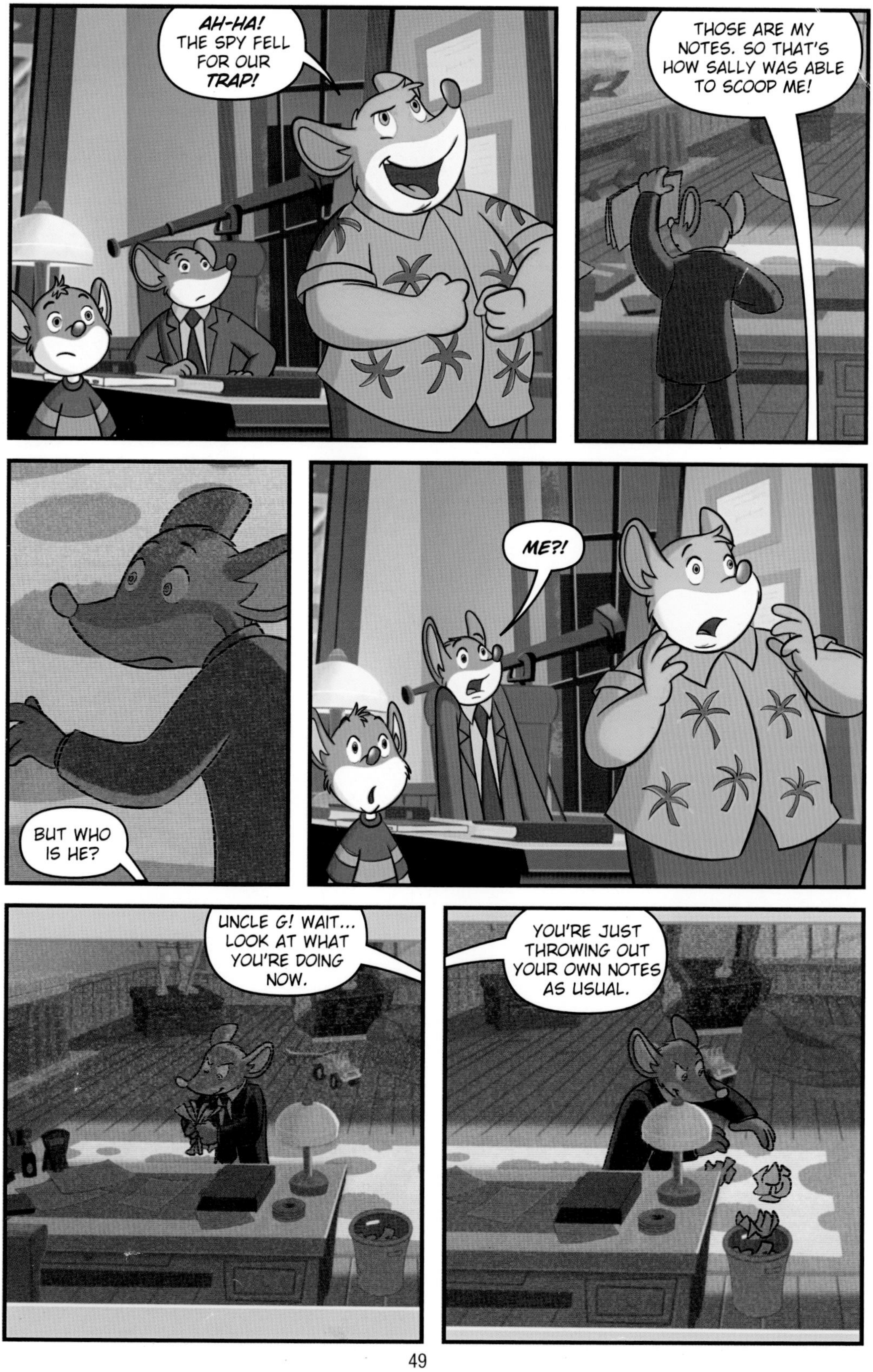
AH-HA! THE SPY FELL FOR OUR TRAP!
THOSE ARE MY NOTES. SO THAT'S HOW SALLY WAS ABLE TO SCOOP ME!
BUT WHO IS HE?
ME?!
UNCLE G! WAIT... LOOK AT WHAT YOU'RE DOING NOW.
YOU'RE JUST THROWING OUT YOUR OWN NOTES AS USUAL.

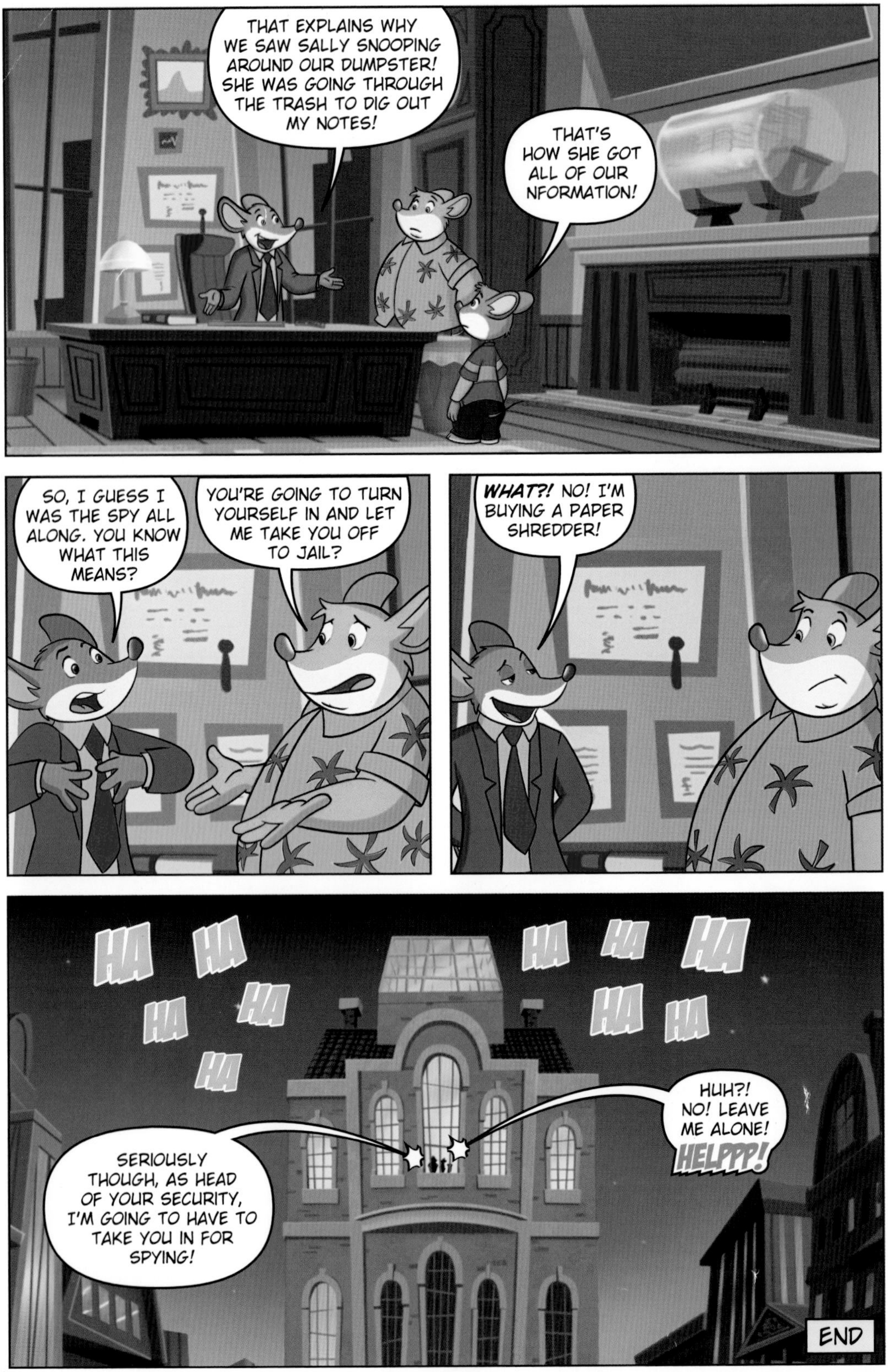
THAT EXPLAINS WHY WE SAW SALLY SNOOPING AROUND OUR DUMPSTER! SHE WAS GOING THROUGH THE TRASH TO DIG OUT MY NOTES!
THAT'S HOW SHE GOT ALL OF OUR NFORMATION!
SO, I GUESS I WAS THE SPY ALL ALONG. YOU KNOW WHAT THIS MEANS?
YOU'RE GOING TO TURN YOURSELF IN AND LET ME TAKE YOU OFF TO JAIL?
WHAT?! NO! I'M BUYING A PAPER SHREDDER!
HA HA HA HA HA HA HA HA HA HA HA
SERIOUSLY THOUGH, AS HEAD OF YOUR SECURITY, I'M GOING TO HAVE TO TAKE YOU IN FOR SPYING!
HUH?! NO! LEAVE ME ALONE! HELPPP!
END

Watch Out For PAPERCUTZ™

Welcome to the sensational, scoop-filled second GERONIMO STILTON REPORTER graphic novel, "It's My Scoop," the official comics adaptation of the second episode of Geronimo Stilton Season One, written by Tom Mason and Dan Danko, brought to you by Papercutz—those lovers of a free press dedicated to publishing great graphic novels for all ages. I'm Salicrup, *Jim Salicrup,* the nit-picky Editor-in-Chief and Geronimo's notes-shredder (They don't call us Papercutz for nothing!).

If you're just joining us, allow me to explain that this is the latest GERONIMO STILTON graphic novel series from Papercutz. The first, simply called GERONIMO STILTON, focused on Geronimo's adventures saving the future, by protecting the past—usually from the those pesky Pirate Cats. That hardcover series is being collected in paperback collections entitled GERONIMO STILTON 3 IN 1, three volumes at a time. This series, GERONIMO STILTON REPORTER, focuses on Geronimo's adventures in the present, where's he's Editor-in-Chief of *The Rodent's Gazette* and its star reporter. In our previous volume you met Geronimo's nephew, Benjamin Stilton, Geronimo's cousin, Trap Stilton, and Geronimo's sister, Thea Stilton. In this volume we meet another character who will play an important role in this series: Sally Ratmousen, the publisher and star reporter of *The Daily Rat*, who also appears on TV with her exclusive "Sally Scoops." And that brings us to "It's MY Scoop!"…

To get a Smurftastic idea of how newspapers started, I suggest checking out THE SMURFS #25 "The Smurf Reporter." You'll see a sped-up mini-history of how journalism, in some cases, has gotten far more concerned with gossip and "breaking news." In "It's MY Scoop!," we see that even Geronimo gets sucked into having to compete with *The Daily Rat* on such stories as revealing the identity of the "Secret Celebrity." The competition is so intense *SPOILER ALERT*, that Sally Ratmousen has her minions digging through Geronimo's trash to steal scoops. Things get so bad that Trap even creates "Fake News" to distract Sally from the real story.

Journalism, like many other noble professions, can be corrupted, betraying its duty to report the truth to the people. Geronimo faces a tough task: maintaining the integrity of *The Rodent's Gazette* as a newspaper that reports the truth, yet keeping it commercially competitive with the less-scrupulous *Daily Rat*.

And some people think comics are never about anything serious… But you know that's not true, especially if you've been following recent Watch Out for Papercutz pages where we've been discussing the Philosophy of Geronimo Stilton as presented at geronimostilton.com. This Philosophy is the guidelines everyone follows in creating GERONIMO STILTON comics, chapter books, and animated TV shows, and it also provides an interesting insight to Geronimo's character and motivations. So without further ado, let's get right to it:

GERONIMO STILTON AND PEACE
In his adventures, Geronimo Stilton always highlights the horrors of war, enhancing the importance of peace. His books want to be reassuring: you have to remember that the future awaiting us is beautiful. His motto is: Instead of being against war, support peace!

Geronimo's right! People tend to get emotional regarding strongly held beliefs, and tempers can flare easily. Violence is not a solution. While it's easy to get mad, it's a lot more challenging to keep calm and find a peaceful solution.

GERONIMO AND COURAGE
Geronimo teaches that confronting your fears is the simplest and most effective way of overcoming them. The best experiences require more effort but make you grow, stimulating you to develop new capabilities. Real courage is not being without fear, but confronting it whilst being aware of your limits and trying to overcome them.

In certain situations, it's perfectly normal to be afraid. And it's never wise to take any unnecessary risks that may cause you or others harm. But, don't ever confuse being nice and decent with weakness. It takes strength and courage to be good and kind. And speaking of which, we want to thank you for picking up this GERONIMO STILTON REPORTER graphic novel. We hope you enjoyed it and that you'll also enjoy GERONIMO STILTON REPORTER #3 "Stop Acting Around," previewed next and coming soon to booksellers and libraries everywhere. And don't miss Geronimo's animated adventures on Netflix and Amazon Prime!

Thanks again,

JIM

STAY IN TOUCH!

EMAIL: salicrup@papercutz.com
WEB: papercutz.com
TWITTER: @papercutzgn
INSTAGRAM: @papercutzgn
FACEBOOK: PAPERCUTZGRAPHICNOVELS
SNAIL MAIL: Papercutz, 160 Broadway, Suite 700,
            East Wing, New York, NY 10038

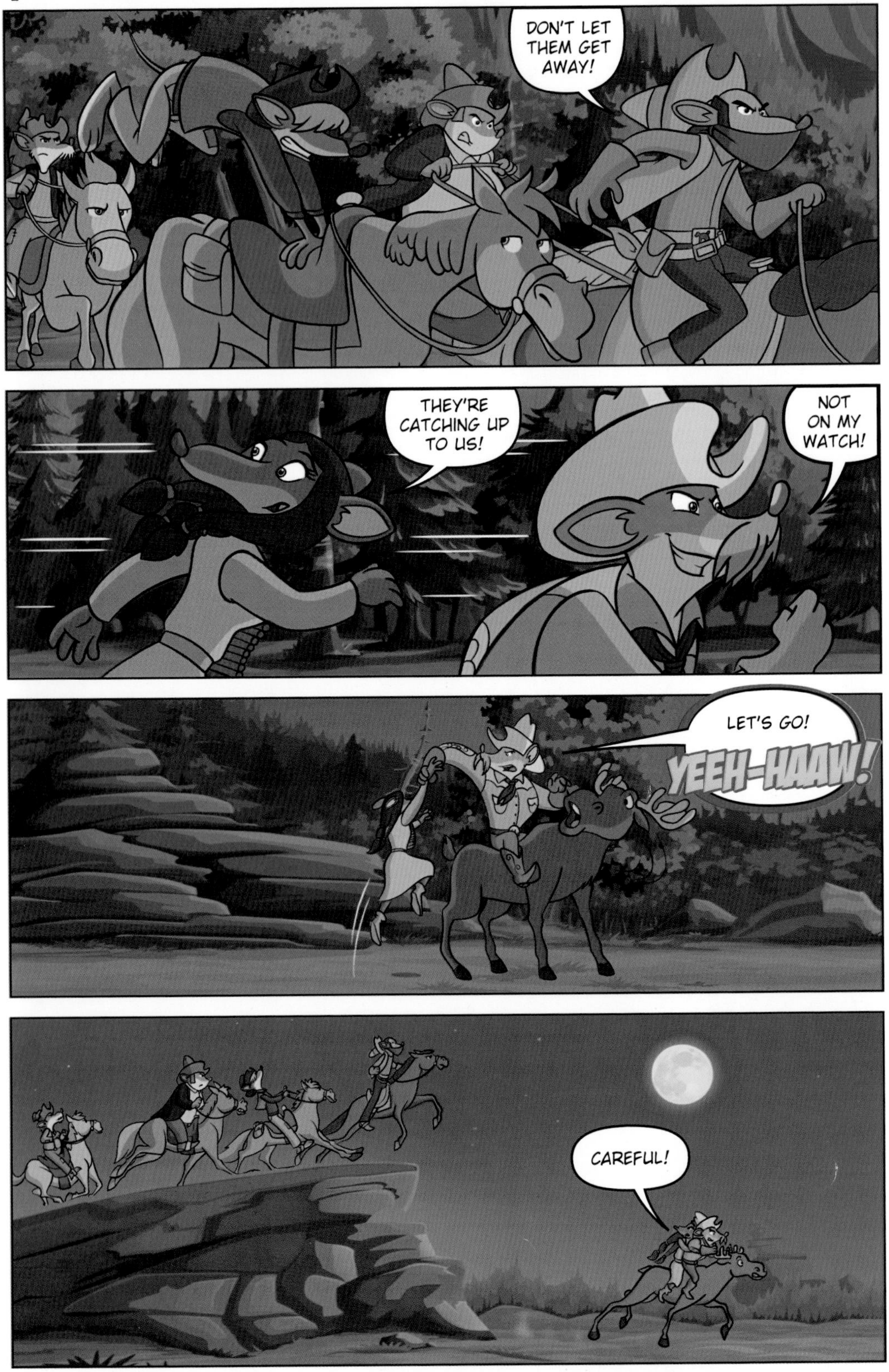
DON'T LET THEM GET AWAY!
THEY'RE CATCHING UP TO US!
NOT ON MY WATCH!
LET'S GO!
YEEH-HAAW!
CAREFUL!

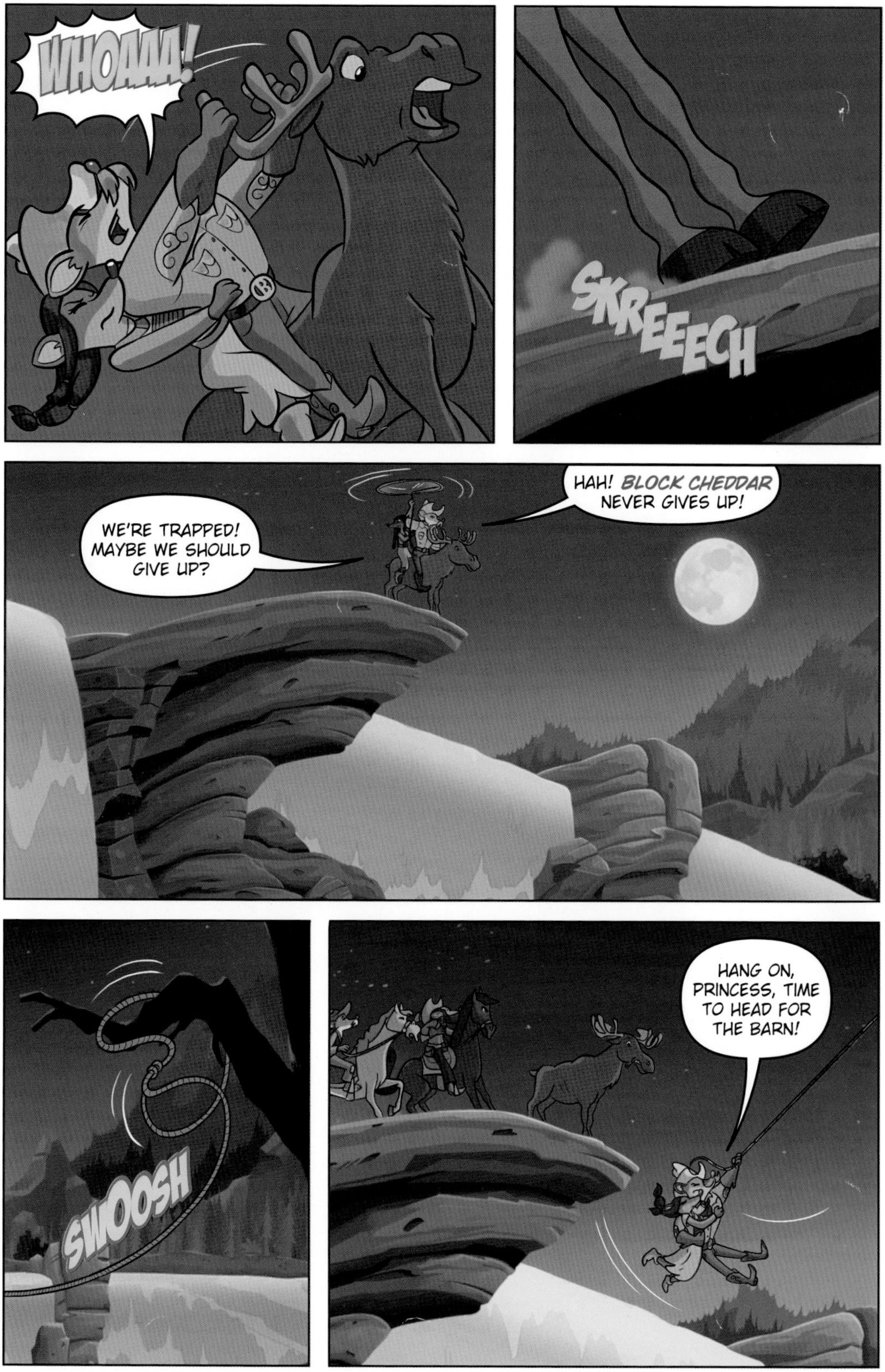
WHOAAA!
SKREEECH
WE'RE TRAPPED! MAYBE WE SHOULD GIVE UP?
HAH! BLOCK CHEDDAR NEVER GIVES UP!
SWOOSH
HANG ON, PRINCESS, TIME TO HEAD FOR THE BARN!

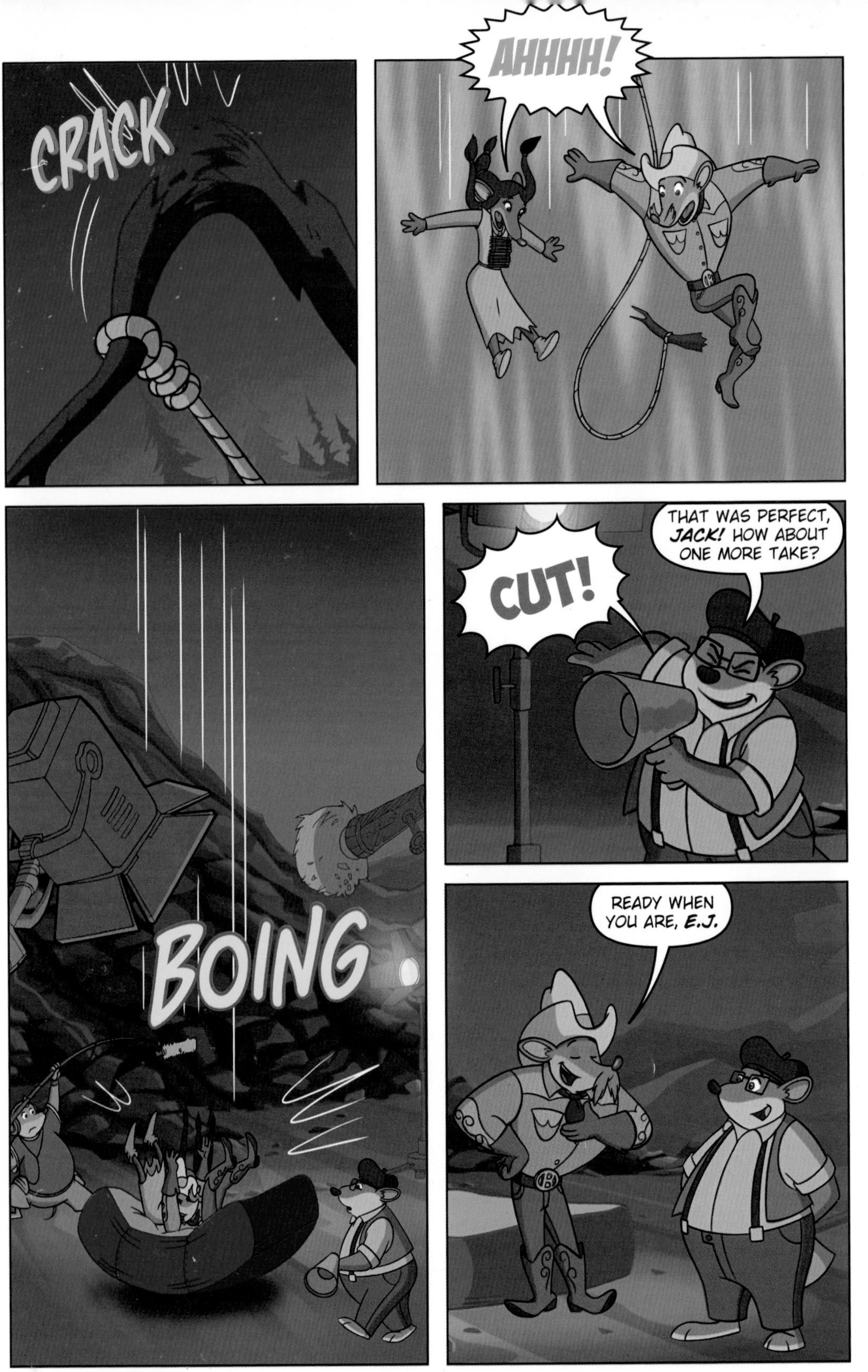
CRACK
AHHHH!
BOING
CUT!
THAT WAS PERFECT, JACK! HOW ABOUT ONE MORE TAKE?
READY WHEN YOU ARE, E.J.

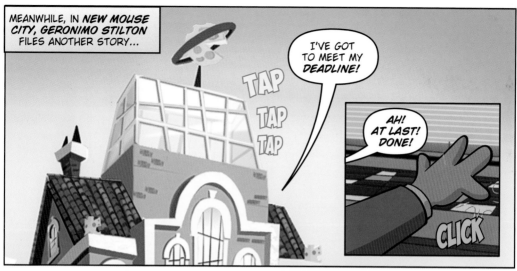

MEANWHILE, IN *NEW MOUSE CITY,* GERONIMO STILTON FILES ANOTHER STORY...

TAP TAP TAP

I'VE GOT TO MEET MY *DEADLINE!*

AH! AT LAST! DONE!

CLICK

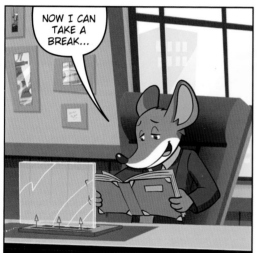

NOW I CAN TAKE A BREAK...

GERONIMO! HOW'S MY FAVORITE REPORTER?

AAAHH!

A LITTLE DISCOMBOBULATED.

GREAT!

SO, G, HOW'S ABOUT YOU VISIT ME ON THE SET OF MY NEW FILM?!

"BLOCK CHEDDAR 4"

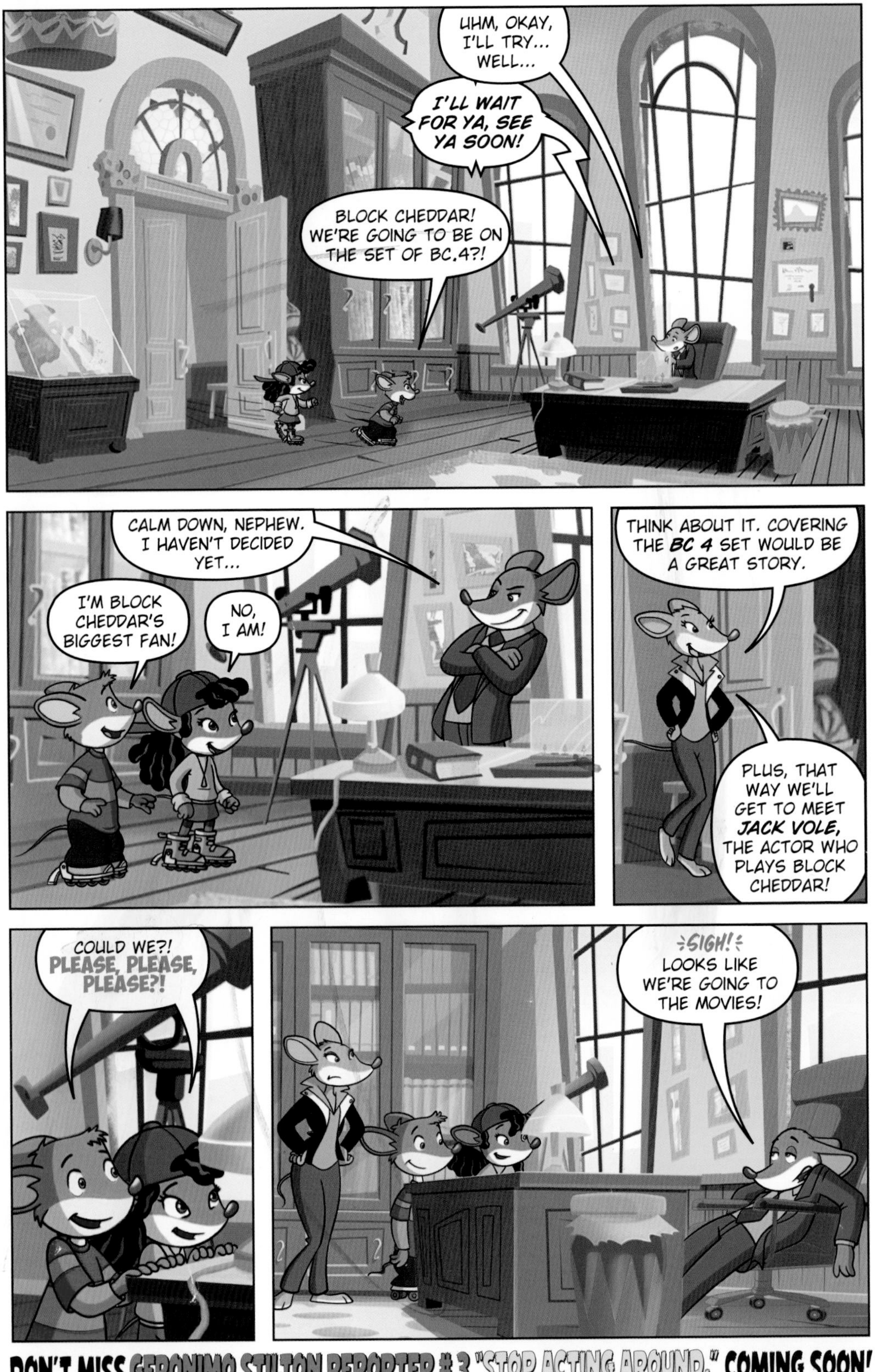
UHM, OKAY, I'LL TRY... WELL...
I'LL WAIT FOR YA, SEE YA SOON!
BLOCK CHEDDAR! WE'RE GOING TO BE ON THE SET OF BC.4?!
CALM DOWN, NEPHEW. I HAVEN'T DECIDED YET...
I'M BLOCK CHEDDAR'S BIGGEST FAN!
NO, I AM!
THINK ABOUT IT. COVERING THE BC 4 SET WOULD BE A GREAT STORY.
PLUS, THAT WAY WE'LL GET TO MEET JACK VOLE, THE ACTOR WHO PLAYS BLOCK CHEDDAR!
COULD WE?! PLEASE, PLEASE, PLEASE?!
SIGH! LOOKS LIKE WE'RE GOING TO THE MOVIES!

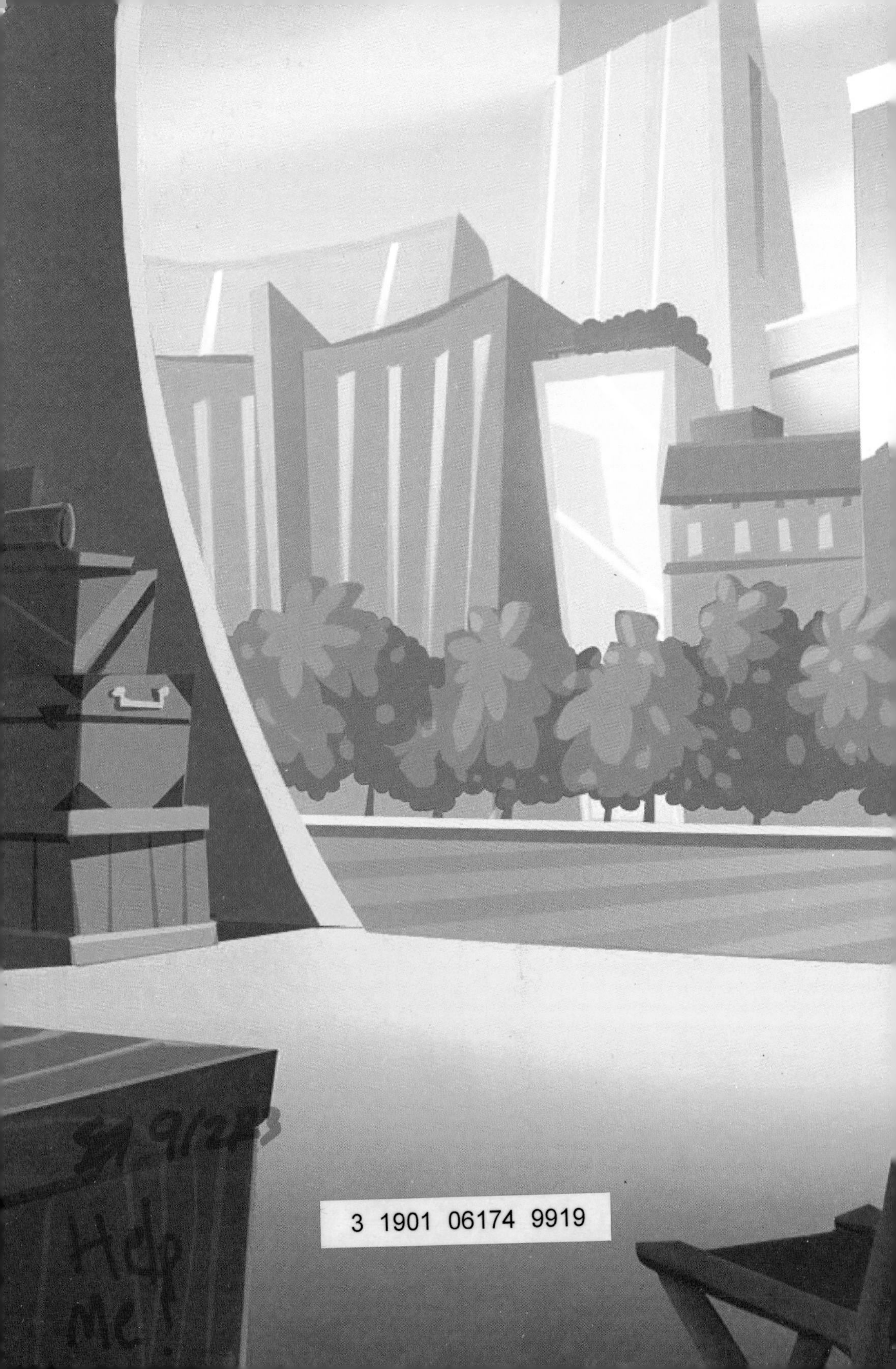
Help me!